MONTMORENCY RETURNS

ELEANOR UPDALE

$\mathcal{A}$UTHOR'S NOTE

It has been a very long time since *MONTMORENCY'S REVENGE*, which ended on a cliff-hanger. Many thanks to everyone who has written to me begging to know what happened next, and my apologies for taking so long to get the next episode into print. I greatly appreciate your patience, and your loyalty.

So here is the fifth book in the series: *MONTMORENCY RETURNS*. It starts where the fourth book left off. As usual, the story is a mixture of real and fictitious events and characters, and as always it doesn't matter if you don't know which are which. A quick search of the internet should reveal all. The mighty Montmorency Falls really exist, and still thunder away in Quebec. If you type 'Edison' and 'film' into a search engine you will be able to see many of the movies mentioned in the text, though not those made by Davy Payne, whose works are lost forever.

I like to think that everything in this book could have happened in 1901/2, but this is a story, and not an historical text. I hope you enjoy it.

Eleanor Updale, 2013

With thanks to Jeremy de Quidt, a gifted writer,
who told me to stop moaning and get on with it.

$\mathcal{C}$ONTENTS

Who's Who

Most of the characters in *Montmorency Returns* appeared in previous *Montmorency* books. New readers may find it useful to read a little background information, and old friends might want to remind themselves of where we left the key players at the end of *Montmorency's Revenge*. But why not just plunge in to the story, and refer back to this section if and when you need to?

MONTMORENCY. Born in London in 1855, he led a life of petty crime until 1875, when he was almost killed during a burglary. On leaving prison five years later, he used the new London sewage system as his base for lucrative robberies – operating under the dual identities of Scarper (a criminal ruffian) and his boss, Montmorency (apparently an admirable member of the upper classes). Although plagued by addiction and identity crises in his early adventures, by the start of this story his friendships with the Fox-Selwyn family and Doctor Farcett have sealed his respectability.

DOCTOR ROBERT FARCETT. Born in rural England in 1852, his early ambition to achieve fame through medical innovation drew him to the injured Montmorency, whose body became an exhibition piece, displaying Farcett's skill. Years later, after Farcett was called in to treat Montmorency's addiction, the two men became friends. Farcett's ambition often led him into trouble. His drive to exploit the new power of X-ray cost the life of his great love, Maggie Goudie, and left him in a state of mental collapse. He had barely recovered when, in September 1901, he became embroiled in unsuccessful attempts to save the life of President McKinley. After that, Farcett retreated to work at the mental hospital in Buffalo, New York, hoping to stay away from excitement.

THE FOX-SELWYN FAMILY. Like most British aristocrats, each member has an assortment of names:

THE DUKE OF MONABURN is Edward Augustus Fox-Selwyn, familiarly known as **GUS.** Born in 1850, He was the twin (but slightly older) brother of Montmorency's great friend, the late Lord George Fox-Selwyn. Gus's first wife died of influenza in 1897. His second, the English-born Italian Contessa, **BEATRICE**, is now the Duchess of Monaburn, and step-mother to Gus's two sons.

ALEXANDER FOX-SELWYN, now the **MARQUESS OF ROSSELEY**, is Gus's elder son. Born in 1879, he is a junior diplomat working at the British Embassy in Washington. Although known in the family for his pompousness, they are unaware that he was involved in undercover work in Italy. He recently married **ANGELINA**, daughter of the police chief in Florence.

LORD FRANCIS FOX-SELWYN – who likes to be known as FRANK – is Alexander's younger brother. Born in 1882, he dislikes the upper-class world in which he grew up. He has been extensively involved in Montmorency's adventures alongside his uncle Lord George Fox-Selwyn, whose death he was determined to avenge. He and Alexander were both with Montmorency during the battle with the Italian anarchist, Moretti, which led to a fire destroying much of the New Jersey town of Paterson.

VI EVANS. Born in 1866, Vi first knew Montmorency on his release from prison, when he stayed at her mother's sleazy boarding house in Covent Garden. Thanks to her friendship with Montmorency, she has risen to become housekeeper, and friend, to the Duke and Duchess.

TOM is Montmorency's son by Vi Evans, although he grew up unaware of his father's identity. Born in 1886, he has spent most of his life on the Scottish island of Tarimond. In 1899, he received a substantial inheritance from Lord George Fox-Selwyn. For much of 1901, he toured in the company of the actor and impresario, Leopoldo Fregoli.

LEOPOLDO FREGOLI was an Italian quick-change artist of international renown. Born in 1867, his fictional life began in 1901, when the Duchess introduced him to Montmorency's world. In real life, his ability to switch identities has given his name to a psychiatric disorder: the Fregoli syndrome.

JERROLD ARMITAGE, born in 1875, is an American diplomat and secret service agent. Once a close friend of Alexander Fox-Selwyn, their relationship has been strained since Montmorency and his friends failed to prevent the assassination of President McKinley.

MARY GIBSON. Born in 1871, Mary is a resident of Paterson, New Jersey, who has won Montmorency's heart.

1. IDNAPPED

Late 1901. A hotel in Paterson, New Jersey, USA

Montmorency was sure there was someone in the room with him. From the corner of his eye he saw the edge of a black cloak. Then he felt the pressure of cold metal against the back of his head. He grasped the arms of his chair, closed his eyes, and tried to feel brave.

In an instant his mind flicked between possibilities. How could this be Malpensa, the anarchist ringleader? Surely he was in jail on the other side of the Atlantic. It must be young Frank Fox-Selwyn, drunk on relief that their enemies had been defeated (and on the liquor at the party downstairs), pulling a stupid, tasteless prank in the hope of shaking Montmorency from his gloom.

"For goodness sake, Frank…" he said, trying to turn his head, but his scolding was cut off as the gun slipped round to the side of his cheek, holding his face forward, so all he could see was the blank wall in front of him and the manuscript on the desk.

"Don't move," said a voice he recognised, but couldn't place. It wasn't Malpensa's bass Italian accent. This was an American. "It's loaded. Stay still, and you won't get hurt."

"What…"

"Don't ask questions. You're coming with me."

Montmorency scanned the desk for anything he could use as a weapon. There was nothing: just an inkwell and the thick stack of paper on which he had written the story of his life.

"Drop the pen," the stranger commanded. This was no joke. But who was this man? Why was the voice so familiar?

The laughter downstairs quietened as Frank started singing a round: "London's burning, London's burning…"

Montmorency's son, Tom, joined in. "London's burning…."

Then Leopoldo Fregoli, the great Italian showman, boomed above the others. Montmorency listened out for Frank's older brother, Alexander, but the next voice to join the song was a high, clear soprano. It was Mary Gibson, the woman for whom Montmorency had written the account of his misdeeds and deceptions, in the hope that she would forgive him and become his wife.

So could it be Alex standing behind him? Surely not. Alexander was the serious one, and after the dangers they had faced together and the deadly tussle that had led to the Paterson fire, he was hardly likely to find a mock execution funny. Alex would even disapprove of Frank's choice of song. No, this was real. But who was the intruder Montmorency had no choice but to obey?

"I said drop the pen," said the man, just as Montmorency was pondering a pathetic attempt to use the nib in his defence. "Now, stand up slowly. Put your hands in the air. If you lower them, I'll use the gun. Watch the wall."

The song below was getting louder, but Montmorency could hear footsteps on the stair. *Alexander. Of course! He'd promised to bring up a plate of supper.*

Montmorency shouted, "Keep out!" But the door creaked open, and he braced himself for a shot. Instead, Alexander's voice broke the tension.

"Jerrold! What the bally heck are you doing here?"

"Armitage?" said Montmorency, still too scared to turn round. "You? Get out, Alex. He's got a gun."

There was a crash of china as Jerrold Armitage knocked the supper tray from Alexander's hands. "Don't try anything, Alex," he snapped. "Stand over there by him. Arms up, and turn around. I'm warning you both. Move and I'll shoot."

Alex started spluttering questions, but Armitage's voice cut through. Montmorency had heard that angry tone before. Jerrold Armitage, an officer in the American secret service, had spoken with the same contempt and rage when Montmorency and Frank had failed to prevent the assassination of President McKinley back in September. But they had made their peace afterwards and, in Paterson, Montmorency had tracked and killed an anarchist, and been hailed as a hero for rescuing hundreds from the blaze that devastated the town. Why was Armitage threatening him now?

"Fire, fire! Fire, fire!" sang Fregoli and his friends. Someone had a drum. Others were stamping out the beat. There was a trumpet and a fiddle. No point in shouting for help. No one would hear.

"I mean it, Alex. Face the wall," said Armitage, as Alexander tried to sneak a look at him. "I've got you both covered. If either of you moves, I'll shoot the other one."

Clever, thought Montmorency. It was flattering, too. Armitage knew that both the men in front of him were brave enough to risk a bullet in their own heads, but too ferociously loyal to endanger each other.

"We're going out through the window," said Armitage, opening it with his free hand. "And don't try to make a run for it. I've got men down there. Do as you're told, and you won't get hurt. You first." He pulled Alexander across the room. "You can drop on to the roof over the lobby, and then swing down the pipe to the ground."

"Do as he says," said Montmorency, realising that they were caught up in a well-planned operation, and fearing heroics that might cost Alex his life.

"Shut up!" Armitage snapped. "Now you. Follow him down."

Armitage turned the key in the lock on the door.

Very professional, thought Montmorency. *They'll all assume I've gone to bed. No one's going to notice I'm missing till the morning. But he should have done it before. Now he's lumbered with Alex as well as me. He can't have planned for that. And why does he want me anyway?*

Armitage pressed the gun into Montmorency's back. "Get a move on," he hissed, lifting the stack of paper from the table, and slipping it into the inside pocket of his cloak.

2. THE MORNING
AFTER THE NIGHT BEFORE

Four shoes lay on the floor of the residents' lounge in the hotel. One, made of fine Italian leather, was under the piano. Its twin was across the room, alongside the sofa. Someone had been using it as an ashtray. Leopoldo Fregoli must have gone up to bed in his socks. The other two shoes, scuffed and dirty, were also lying at odd angles, but they both had feet in them. Frank was snoring where he had fallen after his last glass of bourbon. It was half past ten. The manager had waited as long as he could before letting his staff in to clear away the debris of the party. A maid was struggling to remove an unidentifiable stain from one of the rugs.

Mary Gibson had left long before the party was over. She'd enjoyed herself, but was sad that Montmorency had stayed in his room all evening, and apparently gone to sleep without saying goodnight. She knew he was writing down his life story, and he had warned her that it might contain shocking revelations, but Mary could imagine nothing that would stop her wanting to become his wife. She had slept well, and woken with a warm sense of contentment. After all the dramas of the past few weeks, life was settling down nicely, and though hard work would be needed to help Paterson return to normal, she would relish the effort. She had a purpose, and a quiet confidence that the future would bring her happiness she had hardly dared imagine before.

It was a clear, crisp day, and Mary was glad she had put on her warmest coat for the walk across town to the hotel. She was surprised that Montmorency's window was open. Perhaps the chambermaid was just letting in some air while she tidied his room. Mary was hoping that Montmorency's memoir was finished, and that today might be the day she learned everything about the man with whom she intended to share her life.

Montmorency's son, Tom, waved to her from the hotel lobby, where he was chatting with the bellboy about an article in the local paper. It was yet another feature about the consequences of the huge fire which had left so many Paterson residents homeless. There was a piece about Mary at her soup kitchen, and a rave review of a show put on by Fregoli to raise funds for the victims. Even without the costumes and sets that had been lost in the fire, Fregoli had managed to persuade the audience that they had seen a rich cast of characters, though he had played every one himself. At the end of the performance, when Fregoli had silenced the rapturous applause to announce that he would be leaving the United States in a few days, he had milked the gasps of disappointment with a flourish of an oversized handkerchief that seemed to appear from nowhere.

As Mary entered, Tom called her over to see her picture in the paper. She brushed it away, modestly, and asked whether Montmorency was up.

"I'll go and see," said Tom. But he found the door locked.

"He said he'd help with the lunches today," Mary shouted up the stairs.

"Shall I wake him?" asked Tom, "Or can I give you a hand instead? He must be tired. He's been staying up, writing, every night this week."

Though Mary was anxious to see Montmorency, she couldn't turn down Tom's offer. It would be a chance to spend more time with the young man she hoped would become her stepson. The two of them set off for the centre of town, not looking back to see Montmorency's bedroom curtains fluttering in the icy breeze.

Two hours later, Frank began to stir. He had been dreaming about a transatlantic voyage, and when he stood up he could have believed, from the way the floor was rocking, that he was on board ship. The hotel manager, who was relieved to see the last patch of carpet ready for cleaning, offered to run him a bath. Frank climbed slowly up to the room he shared with Alexander, to collect some fresh clothes.

Alex had reluctantly moved in with Frank when he had arrived in Paterson and found that Fregoli's troupe had commandeered all the rooms in town. This morning, as usual, his camp bed was neatly folded away. After all the drama of the fire, it hadn't taken him long to return to his old, pernickety, ways. Frank assumed that Alex must be up and about somewhere. He couldn't remember seeing much of his brother in the later stages of the party. Maybe he'd taken Mary home, and then turned in for the night. Frank lay back on his own bed, only for a moment, just to get his breath back after tackling the stairs.

He didn't wake again till four o'clock, when Fregoli thumped on his door.

Fregoli had made use of Frank's neglected bathwater and, after a couple of hours in front of a mirror with his hair oil, nail buffer, tweezers and cologne, he was looking spruce and dandy, but he was bored after a whole day without his English friends, and he woke Frank to suggest an early supper. They went to Montmorency's room, but it was locked. After rapping and shouting for a while, Fregoli ambled down to ask the staff whether they knew where Montmorency was. No one had seen him all day.

There could have been a thousand explanations, of course, but Frank couldn't help remembering how depressed Montmorency had seemed the night before – determined not to join in the fun. He persuaded the manager to come up with the pass key, to make sure that all was well. Frank let Fregoli go in first, half dreading that he would find a body on the bed and a suicide note on the desk. But there was nothing. No body, no letter, not even the memoir Montmorency had been writing. None of them noticed the upturned tray and broken china which had been swept behind the door as they opened it.

Fregoli was determined to find a happy explanation for Montmorency's absence. "Maybe he's gone to see Mary – to show her the story of his life, and propose to her properly," he said, as the manager closed the window. "Perhaps you should put some champagne on ice, in case they come back with good news."

The manager smiled. "I'm afraid there's no champagne left, sir, after last night."

"No champagne?" said Fregoli. "It really is time I was on my way home!"

He and Frank went down to the smoking room and played a rather lethargic game of chess until Mary returned. She was with Tom, and had no idea where Montmorency was. The four of them tried to convince each other that there was a perfectly reasonable expectation for his absence, but each of them drifted over to the window from time to time, staring out into the night in the hope of seeing him striding towards the door.

    It had been dark for four hours before Montmorency came back. His clothes were rumpled, and there was a mark on his cheek that looked like a ripening bruise. He wolfed down his supper as if he hadn't eaten all day, but he changed the subject every time someone asked him where he had been, or why Alexander wasn't with him. After thirty-six hours without sleep, Montmorency hadn't the energy to make up a convincing lie, and he couldn't tell them the truth for fear of endangering all their lives.

3. PAYBACK

Climbing down from his bedroom at gunpoint in the dark had been bad enough. There was a time when Montmorency could have done it with ease. In his days as Scarper, the underground thief, or when he had romped around international trouble spots with his old friend Lord George Fox-Selwyn, he could leap and slither his way into and out of all sorts of dangerous situations. But at 46 – and after his battle with the terrorist, Moretti, in the smoked-filled basement of the Paterson library – Montmorency's physical strength and instinctive daring were both on the wane. Armitage had warned him not to try to run away when he hit the ground, but Montmorency never had a chance to flee. There were, indeed, secret service men waiting outside the hotel. One grabbed Alexander before he had even reached the bottom of the drainpipe. Alex was coshed, gagged and handcuffed while Montmorency was still on the roof.

"Wait! There's another one," Armitage shouted from behind him, and Montmorency felt a brief surge of hope, with a flicker of his old courage. The team on the ground was expecting a single prisoner. The rough treatment Alexander received had been meant for Montmorency himself. Perhaps he could get away after all? But he heard rustling in the bushes, and, looking down, he could see that the rectangle of light cast across the ground from the party room framed a dark silhouette in the shape of a man.

Armitage was close behind Montmorency now, with one hand against his shoulder, using his captive to steady himself as he shuffled across the slates. Montmorency's foot slipped, and they both slid down to the edge of the roof. They were only one storey up now, perched above the hotel entrance, but the drop, or what might be the fall, looked like a long way. Montmorency felt with his foot for the gutter, and traced his way to the downpipe. Praying that Alexander's weight hadn't loosened it, he swung himself across and clambered down, straight into the arms of the shadowy figure below. Before Jerrold Armitage hit the ground, Montmorency's hands were tied.

"Good work," Armitage whispered to the man, who had pulled off his own scarf to gag Montmorency's mouth.

Through the window, Montmorency could see his friends bobbing about as they tried to keep the round going: *Fire! Fire! London's burning! Fetch the engines! Pour on water!* Frank was emptying a jug over Tom. Fregoli was using a coal scuttle as a fireman's helmet. No one was looking out of the window to see Montmorency's own belt used to strap his legs together. Then Armitage threw his cloak over Montmorency's head. Everything went black. He was dragged though some bushes. He could smell horses. Two pairs of hands grasped him from above and hauled him over what he took to be the tailboard of a cart. He was thrown to the floor next to what he at first thought was a heavy sack. But it was warm. It was Alexander, unconscious, and barely breathing. Armitage and the other man jumped aboard. With the crack of a whip, and a whinny from one of the horses, the wheels began to roll.

For a while, although he couldn't see through the thick cloth of the cloak, Montmorency could work out where they were: descending the hill from the hotel to the town, on the cobbles alongside the biggest silk factory, mounting the slope up to the waterfall, and passing the grand mansion of Harrison

Bayfield, the richest man in Paterson. But soon they were in unfamiliar territory, and Montmorency lost his sense of direction as the road twisted and looped round on itself. For what seemed like hours he listened hard for any conversation between his captors, hoping for clues as to why he had been snatched from his room, but nobody spoke until Alexander started to stir.

"Gag him," snapped Armitage. "And find him a blindfold. We're nearly there."

Although Montmorency was scared about what might happen next, he was glad to hear that he might soon have the chance to stretch his legs. His right calf was rigid with cramp, and his ribs hurt from resting against something hard. He didn't know that it was his own manuscript, inside the pocket of the cape. He and Alexander were carried from the cart like rolls of carpet. Someone knocked on a door in a rhythm that must have been a code. From the depth of the sound, and the long creak of the hinges, Montmorency guessed that this was a substantial building. The smell of furniture polish and gravy suggested a house rather than an office. His body was dumped in front of a hearth. The sudden heat reminded him of his fight with Moretti in the burning library. He had thought then that he was going to die and, judging by what Frank and Alex told him later, he almost had. They had dragged him out of the inferno and revived him. The mix of panic and strength Montmorency had felt in the burning library returned along with frightening images from that night, but there was no prospect of rescue now. Why was he being treated like this by people who were supposed to be on his side?

He tried to wriggle against the rope and belt that bound him, and a large foot came down on his head, sending a shaft of pain through his eye socket.

"That's enough," said Armitage, as another boot struck the small of Montmorency's back. "Cover the door."

There was one more kick. "That's for Beck," said a low voice. Then Montmorency heard his assailant walking away. He flinched at the sound of someone else approaching, but this time the touch was less rough. The cloak was lifted from Montmorency's head, and as his eyes grew accustomed to the light, he could make out Armitage bending over him and, across the room, Alexander, tied to a chair, struggling against his handcuffs and gag. They both tried to speak, but neither could understand the other's muffled shouts.

Armitage pulled Montmorency into an armchair beside the fire.

"I expect you're wondering why I have brought you here," he said, with almost comic understatement.

Montmorency raised an eyebrow, and mumbled something unintelligible through the tight scarf round his mouth.

"I'll unbind you in a minute, but first I want you to know that there's no point trying to escape. This house is totally secure."

Montmorency looked round the room. Armed men stood in front of each of the windows. The burliest of them – the man who had kicked him – barred the way to the door, watching Montmorency with loathing.

Armitage continued: "I need you to help with a matter of national security – for both our countries. This isn't a request. It's an order."

Alexander spluttered again. Montmorency knew he must be trying to say that Armitage couldn't command them to do anything. They were British citizens, and Alexander, as a member of His Majesty's diplomatic service, should be treated with particular respect.

Armitage ignored him. "It's Malpensa," he said. "He's here, in the United States."

Both Montmorency and Alexander started grunting now. They were certain that Malpensa was under lock and key in Britain. Armitage untied Alex's gag. As Montmorency had expected, Alex started ranting about his diplomatic status. When his own mouth was free he tried to put Armitage right.

"Malpensa's been caught," he said. "Alex had a coded telegram from Britain. That's why he came to Paterson – to tell us the good news."

"Old news," said Armitage. "And false news, as it's turned out. There was a mistake. The Brits arrested the wrong man, and while their eye was off the ball, Malpensa was on his way across the Atlantic."

Alexander was still outraged, leaping to his feet. "So what? Even if you are right, how does that explain the way we have been treated tonight? What's it got to do with us anyway?"

Armitage pushed him back into his chair. "For a start, I didn't come for you, remember? It was Montmorency we needed. He knows Malpensa. None of our men has ever seen him."

Montmorency spoke, still processing the wave of confusion and fear that had hit him at the news that his old adversary might be on the loose again. "But why manhandle me like an enemy? Why rough us up?"

"I'm sorry about that," said Armitage, glancing at the agent by the door. "Things may have gone a little too far. But my men have understandably strong feelings about what your British police did to one of their colleagues. He was mistaken for Malpensa and almost lost his life."

"Beck?" said Montmorency, remembering the name uttered by the man who had kicked him.

"Yes, his name is Miles Beck. He's one of our best men – quite possibly our greatest expert on European anarchists. But he may never be fit for work again. That's another reason we need you."

Alexander was still angry. "But you could have approached Montmorency without all this fuss. You should have asked for his help in the normal way – through the usual channels. If you'd come to me, I could have arranged a civilized conversation in a suitably discreet location. I take it you have informed the British Embassy that Malpensa might be in the country?"

"No. It was important for me to get to Montmorency first, before he heard from any other source that there had been a mistake in Britain. To be honest, we were afraid that your own family might have got a message to you, Alex, but it seems you left your office before it arrived."

"What if they *had* told us?" said Alexander, wondering as he spoke whether his private correspondence was being monitored by the US secret service.

"I had to stop Montmorency setting off on some personal crusade against Malpensa. We've seen what he and your brother Frank can get up to when they're not being properly scrutinised. They could so easily disrupt our mission, just as they went too far in Paterson. You must be able to see that Moretti would have been more use to us alive than dead…"

"Now, steady on!" said Alexander, who understood Armitage's point, but wanted to spell out why, in the thick of a fight, that terrorist had had to die.

Armitage took no notice of his protest, and carried on talking. "And who can say whether President McKinley would still be alive if Montmorency and Frank hadn't been distracted in Buffalo by their own desire for revenge? No, I had to get Montmorency away from the rest of you to insist that he must keep the news about Malpensa to himself. We can't risk any hot-headed free-lance antics this time. This is American soil, and the operation is going to be done our way."

"So you want me to leave the country?" said Montmorency, fighting to keep his anger under control. "That's fine by me. There was no need to warn me off with a kick in the face. You can deal with Malpensa. If you insist on taking the credit, good luck to you. I'm not interested in glory. I just want him to pay for what he's done. If you insist on working alone, I'll get out of the way. It's time I went home anyway."

"No," said Armitage, "I don't want you to leave. In fact, I'm going to make you stay. We need you here."

"But if Montmorency's going to go charging off around the United States looking for Malpensa…" Alexander was getting more belligerent, but Montmorency had fallen quiet. He had already guessed what Armitage was going to say next, and he was beginning to realise its profound consequences for his family and friends.

"Montmorency isn't going anywhere," said Armitage. "We're hoping that Malpensa will come to him."

Alexander thought for a second, "You mean you're going to use Montmorency as bait?"

"Not a word I would have used – but yes. Montmorency will be at the heart of our trap. Along with your brother, Frank, of course. I gather from Beck's reports that Malpensa has even more reason to be after Frank. After all, he's lived amongst the anarchists, and pretended to be one of them. In their eyes he's a traitor."

Alexander was still indignant. "If you think Frank is just going to sit around in Paterson, and wait for Malpensa to come his way, you must be sorely deluded!"

"That's why he is not to know that Malpensa is out there, looking for him. That's why I wanted only Montmorency informed that Malpensa is on this side of the Atlantic." Armitage paced the room, his exasperation with Alexander's imperious tone only barely concealed. "You know too, now, Alex. That can't be helped. But I'm warning you. Not a word to anyone. The upside of the shambles in Great Britain is that Malpensa is under the impression that we think he's out of circulation. If he has any contacts in Paterson, he'll have heard that you believe that too. He'll be off his guard. But if word reaches him that we know he's here, he'll be more wary, more difficult to catch. If I hear from my people that you have told your brother, or any of your friends, they will have to be dealt with before they let the secret out."

"What do you mean, 'dealt with'?"

The contempt and determination on Armitage's face as he answered left Alexander in no doubt. "Surely I don't have to spell it out? And I assure you, I will hear. I've got plenty of eyes and ears on the ground in Paterson. If Frank gets wind that Malpensa is in the USA, I will be the first to know. And I'm sure you'll agree that the best way to make your family appear to be in the dark about Malpensa's whereabouts is for that to be the case in actual fact."

Montmorency shared Alexander's rage. He was being commanded to expose his friends – even his young son, Tom – to danger, but was forbidden to warn them. The consequence of doing so would be to place them in yet more peril. He tried to stand, forgetting for a moment that his legs were still bound. He slumped back into his chair as Armitage continued,

"You can't get away, Montmorency. You have no choice. You are going to do this, and you are going to do it our way."

As Alexander continued to complain, throwing out words like 'preposterous', and 'outrage', Montmorency was wrestling between his desire for a peaceful life and a shimmer of nostalgia for the old days. Despite the danger, he had loved working undercover with Alex's uncle, Lord George Fox-Selwyn, who had been cruelly slaughtered by Moretti, probably at Malpensa's command. Now here was a chance to get back at Malpensa – to see him jailed or even killed. Montmorency hated the idea of lying to his friends, but Armitage had him cornered: there was no way out. With a note of resignation in his voice, he said, "All right, I'll do it. To whom will I report?"

"You still don't understand, do you?" Armitage sneered. "You're not part of the team. You're not one of the workers. You're one of their tools. But you won't be alone. No, not for a second. We will be watching you and your little gang at all times." With a sarcastic smile, he added, "My agents are easy to spot. They look just like everybody else. One false move from any of you, and they will know what to do."

Alexander was still arguing: "But what if Malpensa doesn't find out where Montmorency is? You can't keep Montmorency and my brother in Paterson for ever. America's a big place. Malpensa may not even know that Montmorency's here. He might have come to this country for a completely different reason."

Armitage was furious. "Of course he's come for a different reason! When will you people stop thinking that the whole world revolves around you? He intends to strike at the heart of our democracy, and we don't want two presidents dead in one year. You let us down when it came to protecting McKinley. You can play your part in keeping Roosevelt alive by diverting Malpensa from his primary purpose. And as for hearing where Montmorency is – well, you seem to have done quite well at publicising your presence yourselves."

Armitage took a large book from the table, and told a guard to unlock Alexander's handcuffs. Alex opened the album. Pasted on each page were newspaper cuttings about the Paterson fire and the heroic exploits of a group of well-connected Britons who had evacuated the theatre, saving hundreds of lives, and then ministered to the needs of the homeless and traumatised. There were photographs of all of them. Alexander himself (given his proper title, Marquess of Rosseley) was pictured raising money for the relief fund by delivering public lectures in nearby towns, and on another page he was interviewed in detail about his family history. Montmorency and his close friend Mary Gibson were shown at work in their soup kitchen with Frank Fox-Selwyn, helpfully labelled as the Marquess' younger brother.

Armitage held the book out for Montmorency to see. Montmorency realised that Frank, who had maintained a disguise for nearly a year, was now clearly identifiable. Believing that Malpensa was in custody, he had reverted to his real name and stopped blackening his distinctive red hair. Armitage turned the page. There was a picture of Fregoli giving one of his generous benefit performances. Alongside him was a handsome young boy. The caption identified him as Thomas Montmorency. It was the first time Montmorency had seen that name written down. All his life, the child had been known as Tom Evans, using the surname of his mother, Vi, who had brought him up alone, on the island of Tarimond. Now here was evidence that, on the verge of manhood, Tom had accepted Montmorency as his other parent, and had been proud to give that name to the photographer. Montmorency was moved. But Tom's gesture was bound to add him to Malpensa's list of targets.

Armitage picked up on Montmorency's discomfort. "Ah yes – your son. Don't go thinking you can move him out of the way. No shuffling him off back to his mother, or into some rural boarding school. I want you all in one place. A nice big chunk of English cheese to attract a very large Italian rat."

Alexander couldn't resist puncturing Armitage's smugness. "So you've lost him then? Despite all your spies and informants. You've had intelligence that Malpensa's in America, but he's slipped through your fingers. No wonder you're so desperate to lure him out of hiding. It's not going to look good for you, is it, Jerrold, if you let these anarchists outsmart you a second time? Admit it, man. This isn't about saving your president. It's all about saving your job!" For a moment, Armitage was discomfited. Alexander carried on. "And aren't you forgetting something? I have a job too – work I need to get back to. I can't hang around in Paterson indefinitely. The British Embassy in Washington won't stand idly by if I fail to return, I can tell you. And do you seriously think for one minute that I'm going to keep the Ambassador in the dark about an anarchist hunting down British citizens? You must be mad!"

"Not mad," said Armitage, calmly. "A little irritated that you stumbled in when you shouldn't have. A bit exasperated that you are here, when my plan was for you to be as much in the dark as the others. But I'm working on something that may keep you quiet."

"What do you mean?" Alex asked.

"I'm just waiting for a message from Washington. It may take a few hours." He turned to the guards at the window. "Take them downstairs. To separate rooms. Don't let them talk to one another. And don't let them sleep. Wake me if that cable comes through."

Montmorency and Alexander were at last unbound, but the guards took them to two dank storerooms, and made them stand facing the wall with their legs and arms outstretched, slapping them awake at every sign of slumber. The message from Washington didn't arrive till well into the next day.

4. THE DEAL

The two exhausted captives were reunited in the big room. The guards were back at their posts by the windows and door. This time Armitage was seated in the armchair by the fire, looking well-rested and pleased with himself. Alexander and Montmorency were told to stand.

Alex started protesting again. "This really is an outrage. No diplomat should be treated like this. I will be taking the matter up with…"

"Calm down, Alexander," said Armitage. "I have good news for you. You will not be required to stay in Paterson. After all, it's only natural that you should want to be back with your wife…in her condition." Armitage stroked an imaginary pregnant belly in the air above his own stomach.

Alex was flustered. What was this? Was Angelina, his new Italian wife, going to have a baby?

"I have the doctor's report here," said Armitage. "Apparently there is some cause for concern. You'll be anxious to get back to her, no doubt?"

"Yes of course. But if you think my wife's pregnancy will be enough to keep me quiet about the way Montmorency and I have been abused, and how you plan to break the most basic rules of international propriety, you can think again."

"Oh dear," said Armitage, teasingly. "I was hoping it might be sufficient. One wouldn't want anything to happen to a young mother, or her child. But as it happens, there is something else that might make you think again about how much you tell your bosses." He reached down beside his chair and lifted up a sheaf of papers. Montmorency recognised it at once. It was his memoir. The corners of some of the pages were turned down.

"I've had some very interesting reading overnight," said Armitage. He read out a passage from the first page.

"*I am not who you think I am. I did not acquire my wealth nobly, nor without doing some things of which I am now ashamed. This is a full and truthful account of my life. When you have read it, you may make a judgement as to my character, and I will accept the consequences of your decision.*"

Armitage looked up. "I assume that those words are directed towards your lady friend, Miss Gibson," he said. "But I have taken it upon myself to make a judgement about you as a result of what I have read. It wasn't all news to me, of course. Our agents in Great Britain had filled me in on your connections with the Fox-Selwyn family, and your role in tracking down the terrorists behind the bombs in London back in the eighties; but I have to say that all the stuff about the sewers is fascinating. Still, what I really want to concentrate on is this passage here." He jumped to one of the pages with a corner folded over. Montmorency could tell from its place in the manuscript that Armitage was likely to quote something about his time in Florence, when King Umberto of Italy had been assassinated by the anarchist, Gaetano Breschi. It had been the most painful episode in Montmorency's life, culminating in the death of his greatest friend, Alex's uncle Lord George Fox-Selwyn.

Armitage turned to Alexander. "There is some very interesting speculation in here about you," he said. Alexander turned even more pale than he was already, and Montmorency put his head in his hands. "It seems," said Armitage, "that Breschi might not have been killed by his prison guards, after all. Need I go on?"

Alexander shook his head, but Armitage did have something to add. "It would appear that breaking the rules of international propriety is not entirely outside your experience after all." He flicked through the pages of the memoir. "And there's plenty more in here that might embarrass your father and stepmother, incriminate your brother, and sully the memory of your late uncle. Do you really want to expose them to all that for the sake of undermining our mission against the very terrorists who are their enemies? Is it not in their interests that you should return to Washington and say nothing?"

Alexander was silent. Armitage turned to another page of the manuscript.

"And, Montmorency. About your son..." Montmorency was ashamed to admit to himself that while listening to the revelations he hadn't given a thought to what implications the memoir might hold for Tom. "Do you think he would relish the details of his father's past life becoming public – including the background to his own conception which, I have to say, is far from savoury?"

"That document was not written for public consumption."

"Maybe not," replied Armitage, tapping the pages on his knee to make a neat pile, and carefully tucking it under his chair. "But, Montmorency, you are hardly in a position to stop that now. Unless, of course, you and the Marquess here agree to comply with our plans."

Montmorency looked round the room, hoping that one of the agents might have dropped his guard – giving him a chance to grab the manuscript and launch himself through a window and away. Armitage read his mind.

"You might as well give in, Montmorency. There's no way out of here."

"Where is 'here', actually?" asked Montmorency.

"We're still in New Jersey," said Armitage, "Though we're a fair way from Paterson if you were hoping to escape and walk back. Funnily enough, this place gets a mention in your memoir. It's called West Orange."

"I know it," said Montmorency. "It's where Thomas Edison has his factory. It's where Robert found out how dangerous X-rays can be."

"Ah, Robert Farcett," said Armitage. "Your friend who assisted the medical team that failed to save President McKinley. I was coming to him. In fact he is the reason we chose this house as our centre of operations. I perhaps should have mentioned that my men have gone to the hospital in Buffalo to bring him here. No doubt he'll come if he thinks the invitation is from Edison."

"But why?" said Montmorency. "There's no need for Robert to get involved in this Malpensa business. He's safe working at the hospital. And, as your informants have probably told you, he has, in the past, fallen victim to nervous strain."

"Exactly," said Armitage. "And not to put too fine a point on it, his fragility might help keep you two in line. I already knew that you were friends..." he pointed towards the memoir, "Now I know that you owe him your life. You wouldn't want anything to happen to him, now would you?"

"Is that a threat?" said Montmorency and Alexander together.

Armitage smiled. "Yes, gentlemen, I believe it is. And I warn you, we would have no compunction about harming the doctor if it meant our new president would be safer than his predecessor was in Farcett's hands."

"That's not fair!" Alexander cried, realising too late that he sounded like a petulant schoolboy.

Montmorency was calmer. "So you are going to hold him here?"

"No. I am going to send him to Paterson. I intend to persuade him that his medical expertise is needed there – which might, after all be true. I want to have you all in the same place, so I can concentrate my manpower and be ready for Malpensa when he arrives in Paterson."

"If he goes there," said Alexander.

"Oh he will," said Armitage, gesturing towards the album of press cuttings. "If he reads the papers he will be in no doubt where Montmorency is. I will see to that. And meanwhile you, Alexander, will resume your duties in Washington as if you and I had never spoken." Armitage rose to his feet. "You will both be leaving in twenty minutes. Alexander, I imagine you'll be pleased to hear that we will acknowledge your status by driving you to a station in the car. Montmorency, we'll take you in the cart as far as the outskirts of Paterson. You can walk from there. Maybe you would both like to use the bathroom first? Or perhaps, Montmorency, you found the facilities in your room last night rather familiar? Did the atmosphere of containment make you feel at home?"

Montmorency didn't let himself show his annoyance at being reminded of his criminal past. "Aren't we going to wait for Robert?" he asked.

"Good Lord, no," said Armitage. "I want to speak to him in private. I will instruct him to keep the details of our conversation secret from you, and I expect you to do the same. If either of you is heard to mention my name to the other, we will regard our operation as compromised, and take the action of which I have warned you. Now, you'd better be on your way."

Montmorency stepped forward to pick up the memoir from the floor. Armitage got there first, and snatched it away.

"This is staying with me," he said. "And I warn you – I'm fully prepared to use it. It may be one of the best weapons I have."

5. THE SEEDS OF DOUBT

Mary was relieved when Montmorency returned, and she could see that he was exhausted as he ate his supper, but nevertheless she was a little offended when he agreed to her suggestion that she should walk home alone so that he could get some rest. She sensed that something was wrong. She was unconvinced by Montmorency's explanation for his absence. It had been a long time coming, and then turned out to be something that, if true, he would surely have mentioned straight away. He said that Alexander had received a cable telling him that his wife was expecting a baby, and that there were complications. According to Montmorency, Alexander had been so overwhelmed by the news that Montmorency had offered to accompany him to the station to catch a train back to Washington. So great was his concern for his friend that he had decided to ride with him as far as Philadelphia. Even if that were true, how did it explain Montmorency's rumpled clothes, his exhaustion, and the bruise on his face?

Tom, Frank and Fregoli had been diverted by the news of Angelina's pregnancy, chatting about what the baby might look like, and which names might suit an Anglo-Italian child. They didn't seem to notice that Montmorency wasn't joining in. But Mary had been hoping, even expecting, that this would be the day when Montmorency gave her the written account of his life.

Instead, he had not even mentioned it. In fact, he had hardly spoken to her at all before taking wearily to the stairs.

On her walk home, Mary winnowed out the likely causes of Montmorency's behaviour. The most probable seemed to be that he had changed his mind about the future: that writing the memoir had convinced him they should never wed. Perhaps he had even destroyed the manuscript. Maybe he'd considered doing away with himself. That could explain both his bedraggled physical state and his mood.

Head down, swathed in gloomy thoughts, Mary strode across town. She was passing the burned-out General Store when two youths stepped out in front of her.

"Nice evening," said the taller of the pair, standing a little too close.

It was a moment before Mary realised that she might be in danger. She recognised the tall lad. She had seen him queuing at the soup tent along with other victims of the fire. She was about to say that yes, it was a fine night, when the other boy held up a penknife.

"Give us your money, and you won't get hurt," he said.

Mary had no cash with her. The pockets of her coat held only a handkerchief and the key to her house. As her reactions speeded up she imagined the boys marching her at knifepoint to her door, and then ransacking the place.

"Come on, pass it over," said the tall one, holding out his hand.

Mary opened her mouth to explain that she had no money to give, but not a sound came out. She knew she should try to run, but her feet seemed leaden. She at last understood the expression 'paralysed by fear'.

Then the look in the boys' eyes turned from menace to fright, as a voice came from behind her.

"Are these young men troubling you, ma'am?" The attackers ran off as a large, well-dressed man drew up on Mary's right.

When the boys had gone, he raised his hat. "Forgive me, I felt I had to intervene," he said.

"No. Thank you, sir," said Mary, now quite flustered, and thinking herself stupid for insisting on walking home alone.

"I'll see you to your door," said the stranger, without introducing himself, and the two of them walked together for half a mile or so till they reached her house. They exchanged pleasantries about the weather, and Mary repeatedly insisted that she was unaffected by the little drama, which she put down to youthful high spirits. She said she knew the boys, which wasn't strictly true.

It was only later, alone at home, that Mary had an odd feeling about her rescuer. As she checked that her maid had left the windows securely fastened, she realised that he had neither given his name, not asked any questions about her. And yet he had led her to her front gate without having to ask the way. She had no recollection of meeting him before. Perhaps he was just a good Samaritan in the right place at the right time. Thank Heaven he was passing. She spent a fitful night imagining what might have happened had he not been there.

By morning, Mary had decided not to tell Montmorency about the incident. She didn't want to make him feel bad for failing to escort her across town. But, as they doled out soup that lunchtime, she did tell Frank, asking him to look out for the boys who had attacked her. She talked about the helpful stranger, too – how he had appeared from nowhere at the crucial moment, and taken her safely home. Frank agreed that she had been very lucky.

Montmorency, stacking bags of potatoes outside the tent, heard every word. As Mary had predicted, he felt awful about letting her walk home alone. But he was pretty sure that the stranger hadn't been on the scene by accident. Armitage's agents must be watching them already. He was hurt that Mary was keeping something from him, even if she thought it was for his own good. But of course Montmorency was hiding something much bigger from Mary. This wasn't the partnership of utter honesty they had promised each other before Armitage and Malpensa had re-entered his life.

While the others were at the soup kitchen, Tom was helping Fregoli at the hotel. Most of Fregoli's costumes and sets had been lost in the fire, and he was writing ahead to his agent in Italy so that replacements would be ready soon after he came home. The list already included the most up-to-date film cameras and projectors. Fregoli was determined to expand beyond the theatre and into the cinema when he got back to Europe. Now he and Tom were compiling instructions for the costumier. Fregoli, patting his expanding belly, admitted that he would need to send new measurements to the seamstress in Rome who had always worked for him. The costumes needed to be loud and flouncy, but they also required all sorts of quick-release fastenings, reversible sections, and special flaps for props, so that Fregoli could act every part in a play without taking too much time to change his clothes. Tom was doing his best with a tape-measure and a sketchpad, but he and Fregoli were not making fast progress with the list. As Fregoli described each garment, he slipped into the personality of the character who would wear it. His whole body changed shape, his voice altered, and little mannerisms aged him into a grandmother, or made his middle-aged body seem like that of a young athlete. Tom copied some of his moves, throwing in impressions of their family and friends: the grandiloquent bombast of the Duke of Monaburn – Frank and Alex's father – who was much cleverer than he liked to make himself appear; Frank's equally mannered attempt at a cockney accent, complete with a swagger and confrontational sneer; Alexander's pompous irritation at his brother's impetuousness; Fregoli's own impish charm.

The showman laughed. "You're good, Tom. You've got a natural gift. If you came on the road with me I could teach you a thing or two."

"I'd like to," said Tom. "But I'm only just getting to know my Dad properly. He's ready to settle down. I think he expects me to stay with him."

"But you're young, Tom. You have your whole life before you. I bet your father wasn't fitting in with other people's plans when he was your age."

"Maybe not," said Tom, who had been told only the sketchiest details of Montmorency's past. "I don't think there was anyone to tell him what to do. I know he didn't have any parents. He was all on his own when he left school. He had to make his own way in the world."

"And how old was he then?"

"About 13, I think."

"So, two years younger than you are now, and he could do as he chose?"

"I suppose so. I hadn't really thought of that. I've been the youngest one around here for so long, it's hard for anyone to believe that I'm old enough to make my own decisions."

"But you are, Tom," said Fregoli. "And take it from an older man: it's the things you don't do that you will regret, not the things you do."

"So will you help me persuade Montmorency to let me go to Italy with you?"

"I'll try. I'll have a word with him tonight."

Between them, they acted out the scene they expected: Fregoli buttering up Montmorency with lavish praise of his son's acting and organisational skills, and Tom doing a perfect impression of Montmorency's voice, begging Fregoli not to deprive him of his handsome, gifted, charming boy in a speech that was almost Shakespearean in tone. They didn't notice Montmorency coming back to the hotel after his stint at the soup kitchen, and lurking at the open door, watching them. The conversation that followed was nothing like the one that had left the bellboy holding his sides with laughter. It was brief, and it was acrimonious. Montmorency was adamant. Tom was to stay in Paterson, and that was that.

6. Afternoon Tea

Armitage had studied the security file on Doctor Robert Farcett, and he knew he must adopt a different approach from the bullying and blackmail that seemed to have worked on Montmorency and Alexander. He had met the doctor before, of course, when (on Alexander's suggestion) he had recruited Montmorency and Frank to watch out for anarchists in the run up to the McKinley assassination. Then, Armitage had regarded Farcett as nothing more than an affable hanger-on, but now he knew more about him, and thought he might be useful. The doctor, brilliant in his way, had a history of emotional weakness. His ambition to make a name for himself through medical innovation had led him to do things he now regretted from the bottom of his soul. The only woman he had ever loved had been killed thanks to his flirtation with the power of X-rays. At least one patient had died in an unnecessary experimental operation.

Farcett's friends had kept his identity secret while he was treated for obsession and despair in a mental hospital in Scotland, but now the American secret service knew all about it. Their agent, Miles Beck, had pieced everything together and sent full details in reports from his semi-retirement in Britain. The Duke and Duchess of Monaburn had unwittingly told him many secrets. They had been shocked to hear that the British police had ill-treated Beck, and felt guilty because they had mistaken him for Malpensa and insisted on his arrest. To make up for their error, they took a close interest in making his convalescence as comfortable as possible. Beck had been invited to Glendarvie Castle in northern Scotland, and in the relaxed atmosphere of country life he had listened well – extracting information without seeming to pry. Montmorency's memoir had corroborated and expanded the impression that Beck had passed on to Armitage: with George Fox-Selwyn dead, Doctor Robert Farcett was the most important man in Montmorency's life, and Montmorency was likely to do everything in his power to protect him.

After President McKinley's assassination, Farcett had stayed on in Buffalo, studying the latest psychiatric theories in the Romanesque splendour of the city's grand mental hospital, the State Asylum for the Insane. In a letter to Montmorency (intercepted by one of Armitage's men) he had declared that he'd found his spiritual home at last. Armitage knew he would have to use all his persuasive skill to tear Farcett away and get him to Paterson, but Montmorency himself had unwittingly made the task a little easier. In his reply (also intercepted) he had given a graphic account of life in Paterson after the fire, including a paragraph on how overstretched the medical facilities had become. He hadn't appealed to Robert to come and help, but it was the next best thing.

Armitage, however, wanted to talk to Farcett first, and he needed to lure him from New York State to New Jersey without delay. That was why Armitage had taken the liberty of using notepaper belonging to the great inventor, Thomas Edison. He hadn't risked imitating Edison's handwriting, but had issued an invitation on his own behalf, explaining that he was a guest in a house owned by the scientist. He heavily implied that Edison particularly wanted Farcett to come, for a reason that couldn't be mentioned in a letter. The story was a little clumsier than he would have liked, and given more time he might have come up with something more robust, but Armitage hoped it would sound intriguing rather than suspicious. He had primed the two agents sent to collect Farcett from the station with facts about Edison's latest enterprises in the motion picture business, so they could chat with him on the way to the house. It worked, and Farcett arrived relaxed – and credulous.

Edison himself knew nothing of all this (Armitage had arranged for him to be called away on business) but as Farcett settled into the same armchair in which Montmorency had sat, bound and gagged, the night before, Armitage passed on the inventor's apologies, pretending Edison had asked him to take on the role of host.

"He's so sorry to miss you. There's some sudden drama in New York about a rival who's infringed one of his patents. There wasn't time to stop you setting off, I'm afraid, but I hope you won't feel your journey was wasted. Edison has told me to carry on as if he were here." Armitage poured out two cups of strong tea. "When he heard that we'd met before, he was most anxious to bring us together again. Sugar? He's says you've written the most fascinating letters about your psychiatric studies in Buffalo."

Farcett shrugged modestly at the suggestion that Edison might admire his work. Stirring his tea, he asked, "Tell, me, how did you get to know Edison? I was under the impression that your interests were – how shall I put it – political, rather than scientific."

"Indeed," said Armitage, pleased to see that Farcett was instinctively cautious about putting a 'secret service' label on his work, even when they were alone together. "You know of course that I have been closely involved in the investigation of the President's assassination?"

Farcett nodded, and Armitage continued, "Well, it turned out that representatives of Edison's cinematographic company were filming at the Pan-American Exposition in Buffalo on the day McKinley was shot. It was my job to look through all the film in case there was any new evidence: signs that the gunman hadn't acted alone – that sort of thing. Alas, there were no images of the shooting itself, but there is a record of the President's last ever speech, and extensive coverage of the crowds. My men and I have been examining the faces for known agitators."

"And while you've been here, you have got to know Edison himself?"

"Quite so," Armitage lied. "He kindly loaned us this house, and I am pleased to say he has visited often. Somehow your name came up, and he suggested that, in view of your interest in psychiatry, we should meet. He felt you could be of invaluable assistance in my next project."

"Which is?"

Armitage looked round, as if to check that the two of them were truly alone. "Looking more deeply into the motivation of the President's killer, and of those who espouse his anarchist ideals. We know they have political aims, of course, but we are also interested in what makes their recruits find that view of the world so appealing. It seems to us that personal trauma or deprivation may open them up to manipulation by charismatic leaders." Armitage waved a hand in the air, as if dismissing his own idea. "But we are only amateurs, of course."

"No, no. You have a point," said Farcett, "But there are people far more qualified than I who could explain how anarchists' minds work. I'm a generalist. A dabbler, really."

"Ah, but if we were to send in some mad professor with a notebook, we would be blowing our own cover straight away."

"Send in? Where?"

"You'll have heard of Paterson, of course."

"I stayed there, briefly, in '99, when I was on my way here to meet Edison for the first time. My friend, Montmorency – you'll remember him…"

Armitage responded casually. "Naturally, and anyone who's read the papers recently can't fail to have heard all about his involvement in the fire."

"Yes. Well, of course you know he's there. Montmorency has been keeping me up to date with events in the town. They're having the devil of a job caring for all the people who lost their homes."

Armitage leaned across the tea things, dropping his voice to embrace Farcett in confidential information. "Well, as you know, Paterson has been a hotbed of political trouble in the past. We like to think that we have cleared out all the old terrorists, but what intrigues us is whether new hotheads are rising from the ashes, as it were."

"And you want me to find out?" said Farcett.

"Exactly. But it would seem suspicious if you just arrived from nowhere asking questions. No. What we have in mind is for you to go there to deal with the general medical requirements of the population…"

"Oh, they are urgent. Montmorency wrote to me the other day with the most harrowing account of unmet need."

"Did he?" said Armitage, betraying no sign of having read the letter in transit. "So for you to go to Paterson apparently in response to his words would not seem strange?"

"Not in the slightest. In fact, I had been contemplating a visit to Montmorency anyway."

Armitage was glad to see the enthusiasm in Farcett's eyes. He continued, "Because, if you were to take on the study I have mentioned, I would require you to keep it secret – even from someone as trustworthy as Montmorency. The findings would be worthless if our subjects knew they were being observed. Do you think it would be possible for you to hide the true nature of your interest?"

"I can keep my mouth shut, if that's what you mean. It's part of the armoury of the medical man. Confidentiality is a cornerstone of our profession."

Armitage thought of the ease with which his agents had been able to find out about the gynaecological status of Alexander's wife, but he said nothing to contradict Farcett. "Precisely. That's something our two trades have in common. And, like me, you'll know that when secrets get out it's usually the result of a harmless remark, passed between friends, that's told and retold quite casually, always 'just between ourselves' of course."

"Which is why it's better to say nothing in the first place," Farcett added.

"We understand each other. It's obvious that you're the man for us. You will appreciate that it might be difficult for our government if it became known that citizens of the United States were, in a sense, being spied upon."

"But this isn't really spying."

"Indeed not." Armitage smiled. "Shall we call it 'research'?"

"That's how I shall regard it. Confidential research."

"Do you want more time to consider my proposal, or can you give me an answer now?" Armitage asked.

Without even a beat for thought, Farcett said, "Yes, I'll do it." And at once his mind was racing ahead to how he would structure his study, and what he would have to do to make sure that no suspicions were aroused.

Seeing he was on receptive ground, Armitage jumped in with a final, crucial demand. "And one more thing. I ask you, please, to stay in Paterson once you are there. Make sure everybody knows and trusts you. Don't let them think you are just an observer popping in and out. Really get dug in. Become part of Montmorency's little gang, of which the city has become so proud."

Farcett smiled, remembering an old Scottish expression he had picked up on the island of Tarimond. "I'll be a kenspeckle figure," he said.

"Splendid. I don't know what that means, but it sounds just fine. I will give you an address at which you can contact me with your findings. A letter every couple of days should suffice. Unless there is anything urgent, of course."

"So you won't be here, in this house?"

"No. My work here is done, alas. I have so enjoyed Mr Edison's company." Armitage threw in Edison's name again as insurance against Farcett getting cold feet, but as he spoke he realised a danger, too, and added. "By the way, this must not be mentioned to him either. We suspect that Edison's mail may be subject to interception by commercial rivals. Best not to correspond at all until this operation is over. I'll explain that to him when he returns from New York, so don't be surprised if you hear nothing from him for a while."

Farcett praised his friend. "Do you know, until this afternoon, I had no idea that Edison had any link with your line of business? How good he is at hiding it!"

"Well, model yourself on him, and you won't go wrong," said Armitage, well aware that Edison had no links with the secret service at all. "To anyone you encounter, friend or stranger, you must present yourself simply as a medical doctor, hoping to help the people of Paterson recover from their terrible experience."

"Which will be true, in its way," said Farcett, buttering a tea cake. "It will take me a while to make travel arrangements, of course."

Armitage was firm. "I would rather you went straight away. If you make a list of the things you would like brought on from Buffalo, I can send men to fetch them."

"I have my medical bag with me," Farcett said. "I never travel without it, just in case. I have a change of clothes. I see no reason why I shouldn't go first thing in the morning, especially since Edison is away."

"I know he'll understand, though he will be sorry to have missed you," said Armitage, rising to summon the agent who had been waiting outside the door. It was the man who had roughed up Montmorency the night before. Armitage gave him instructions. "Doctor Farcett will be requiring transport to Paterson. Have the car ready after breakfast." Armitage smiled at Farcett as if to ask whether the timetable suited him, but Farcett could tell that he had no choice; and anyway he was already a little excited at the prospect of seeing Montmorency, Frank and Tom, and of getting stuck in to helping the people of Paterson and finding out how their minds were working.

Armitage had another request for the agent. "Do you think you can get a couple of those films set up to show Doctor Farcett after supper?" It sounded like a casual request to prepare an evening's entertainment. Farcett wasn't to know that the impromptu cinema session would involve three agents climbing two walls and breaking in to a secure stock room.

Late at night, Armitage and Farcett sat in the dark watching silent pictures of President McKinley greeted by crowds for the last time. There were other films: all of them very short, mainly of landscapes, cars and railway trains. As they emptied a whisky bottle, they watched one reel several times. It showed a lady gradually disrobing as she swung on a trapeze.

By the end of the evening, Farcett had complete trust in Armitage, and could see why his old friend, Edison, had taken such a liking to the affable security man. He was looking forward to playing his part in sustaining the democratic order it was Armitage's job to uphold. He even felt somewhat flattered, as a foreigner, to be given such an important task. He couldn't wait to get started, and was looking forward to passing on his findings about the political temperature of the people of Paterson.

Next morning, when the doctor had gone, and the agents began stripping the house of any sign of their presence, Armitage congratulated himself on a brainwave he'd had the previous day. Soon after Montmorency had left, Armitage had decided not to tell Farcett anything about Malpensa. It would be enough for Montmorency to believe that his old friend was in the know. If Farcett was in the dark, there could be no risk of him accidentally leaking the news that Malpensa was in America. And who could say – the completely bogus research project dreamed up over the teacups might turn out to be interesting, after all.

7. DEPARTURE AND
ARRIVAL

The foyer of the Paterson hotel was in uproar. Fregoli was shouting in loud Italian to his many assistants, who had collected together those of his possessions that hadn't perished in the fire. Montmorency, Mary and Frank had come home early from the soup kitchen to see him off. His journey would take him to New York for the night, and then across the Atlantic to Naples, where he would prepare for a new tour of European capitals. The hotel manager, slightly surprised that Fregoli had paid his large bill in full (and with a substantial tip), was helping to load the baggage onto carts. As Fregoli grasped Frank's hand, he slapped his other arm, smack on the spot where a bullet fired by Malpensa in Paris the previous summer had smashed the bone. Frank flinched, and the two of them fell into an embrace as they pondered the dangers they had faced together. Mary smiled, allowed Fregoli to brush her cheek with his lips, and thanked him for the fun he had brought to Paterson in its darkest days. Tom stood at the door, watching as Montmorency checked that everything was ready for Fregoli's departure. It seemed to Tom that Montmorency couldn't wait for Fregoli to leave. Tom knew that Fregoli had begged Montmorency to let him go too – the noise of their argument had filled the hotel the night before. But Montmorency had refused to countenance the idea, or to give a credible reason for denying Tom his heart's desire. It seemed even more cruel for Montmorency to do everything in his power to speed Fregoli on his way now.

"Come on, Leo!" Montmorency cried, holding open the door of the carriage. "You can't keep the driver waiting!"

Fregoli ignored him, and embraced the hotel staff one by one, doing quick impressions of some of their mannerisms and, when the manager went off to get the final receipt from the office, impersonating him so accurately that the lobby was rocking with laughter when he came back.

But Tom wasn't laughing, and Fregoli caught his eye. He strode towards the boy and drew him into the folds of his long fur coat, muttering something in Italian. Tom had no idea what he was saying, but he knew that the only place he wanted to be was with Fregoli and his team, rattling towards the big ocean liner and a future of quick-change routines and applause. He toyed with the idea of jumping on the cart and hiding amongst the panniers and trunks, but Montmorency, stiff and stern, was watching him, and Tom knew it was hopeless: he would have to stay.

Tom wasn't the only one who was crying as the carriages rolled down the hill and turned out of sight, but the others composed themselves in minutes. Tom's tears wouldn't stop, and when Montmorency tried to comfort him, he shook his arms away and kicked out with a hiss of incomprehensible snot-drenched abuse. Mary tried to intervene, but all she got was an indignant sniff as Tom turned, stomped upstairs, and slammed his door.

"You should have let him go," said Frank.

Montmorency snapped back, "Don't you start."

"But what is there for him here? It's not as if it's his home."

"It is for now. And it might be forever," said Montmorency, looking across to Mary.

"It's still a dump," sneered Frank.

Mary put her head in her hands.

"Apologise!" said Montmorency. "We're guests here."

"Prisoners more like!" Frank said. "How much longer are we going to stay?"

"As long as we are needed," said Montmorency. "If you feel you can turn your back on those people we were helping today, you're a lesser man than I took you for."

Frank was taken aback by the ferocity of Montmorency's reply. Mary intervened. "I think everyone's getting a bit over-wrought. We're all sad that Fregoli has gone, but let's calm down."

There was a moment of silence. They looked at each other in exhausted sulkiness, each of them realising that, without Fregoli, Paterson was going to become a very different, duller place. Then footsteps on the path were followed by a shout.

"Hello there! I've come to help." Robert Farcett had arrived, carrying his doctor's bag and a small valise.

There was no response.

Farcett dropped his bags and waved, "It's me! Robert! Surely you haven't forgotten me already?" he laughed.

As Farcett walked towards him, Montmorency passed from surprise to pleasure, and then to fear. He hadn't expected Armitage to deliver Farcett into the trap so quickly. His emotions came together in an over-formal handshake that took Robert aback.

Then Frank approached Farcett with genuine warmth. "You remember Mary, of course," he said, beckoning her forward.

"Indeed, but I could forgive her for forgetting me. I was here only briefly, a couple of years ago," said the doctor, shaking Mary's hand enthusiastically. "I have heard a great deal about you since then, Miss Gibson. I hope you will not be embarrassed to learn that you are a major theme in Montmorency's letters."

"I trust he does not criticise me too rigorously," said Mary, with a smile.

"He has not made me aware of any faults, Miss Gibson. I am sure you have none." Farcett turned to Montmorency. "Do you know whether there any spare rooms here?"

"Several," said Frank. "Fregoli and his entourage have just left us. You couldn't have timed your arrival better."

No doubt it was planned for you, Montmorency thought. *Armitage will be pleased that he has at last got us all in one place.* He managed to keep smiling. "Let's get you checked in, Robert, and give you a chance to freshen up."

"And then we can catch up over supper," said Frank. How long are you going to stay?"

"As long as I'm needed," said Robert, waving his medical bag. "I intend to make myself useful."

To Armitage, as much as to us, no doubt. Montmorency looked at Farcett's clothes and face for signs that he had suffered at the hands of one of the agents. There was nothing.

But Farcett had noticed the bruise on Montmorency's cheek. "How did you get that?" he asked, prodding it gently.

Montmorency laughed it off. "A present from a grateful nation! I'll tell you about it later." He took Farcett's gentle laugh as a signal that he guessed what Armitage's men had done. In fact, it was simple politeness from the doctor, in response to a joke he didn't understand.

8. CROSS - PURPOSES

Montmorency wanted a few private words with Robert before supper. He felt the need to establish some ground rules – to make sure that they both had the same attitude to the predicament in which they found themselves. He had no intention of risking Robert's safety by speaking openly, but he was sure they would comprehend each other's real meaning in a conversation that any eavesdropper would assume to be a natural exchange between two old friends. Montmorency knocked on Farcett's door. The room had been Fregoli's and still smelt of cigar smoke.

"Do you have everything you need?" said Montmorency. "You don't seem to have brought much luggage."

"The rest is being sent on. I like to travel light, you know, and it was a bit of a last-minute decision to come."

"I understand," said Montmorency, hoping Farcett would pick up the emphasis in his words.

"Well, I couldn't resist the temptation, after your last letter. I knew I had to offer to help."

Good, thought Montmorency. *He knows that we are being watched. He's not going to risk speaking openly about Armitage even when we think we are alone.*

As if to confirm his judgement, Farcett changed the subject: "She's a fine woman." Montmorency was temporarily thrown. Farcett smiled at his discomfort. "Miss Gibson," he said. "I can already see that you have made a good choice there. I understand why you want to stay in Paterson."

Oh, well done Robert! You really are surprisingly good at this. "Yes I have to stay," Montmorency said aloud, "There is no choice."

Farcett smiled and said, "I'm glad to hear you say that." He patted Montmorency's arm in a gesture that Montmorency interpreted as coded confirmation that he shouldn't put his friends in danger by defying Armitage.

In fact, Robert was thinking of how he had left behind his own love, Maggie Goudie, on the island of Tarimond while he went gallivanting round the World with Montmorency and the Fox-Selwyns. She had died while he was away. Farcett's tone became serious: "Sometimes you have to look deep inside yourself to decide what really matters, and there are occasions when other people are what matters, however great one's own selfish desires."

He's telling me that he's going along with all this too, thought Montmorency. *He knows that Tom, Frank, and even Robert himself will suffer if I disobey Armitage's commands and tell them what is going on.* "But it's hard when one feels unable to speak freely of such matters," Montmorency said.

"I understand," said Robert, who had found it difficult to express his love for Maggie to her, to others, or even – at the time – to himself. He was actually finding this conversation a little embarrassing, too. "No need to go into details," he added, as a tap on the door indicated the arrival of a chambermaid with a jug of hot water, some soap and a couple of towels.

Montmorency had seen the girl a hundred times since he had moved in to the hotel. She had always given him a cheeky smile. Now he found himself looking at her through different eyes. Was she one of Armitage's spies? Had she been listening at the door before she knocked? Had she understood the true import of what they had said? Would she be reporting back on their conversation? At least, if she did, she would put Armitage's mind at rest. Montmorency and Farcett were sticking to the rules. Neither had mentioned Malpensa's presence in the United States, nor their conversations with Armitage himself. But Montmorency now felt comforted by the certainty that one person understood what he had to do, and why. And if Robert could do such a good job of behaving as if Armitage and Malpensa had no hold over him, there was no excuse for Montmorency caving in under the strain. For the sake of all his companions, he would have to be strong.

Half an hour later, Farcett was setting off for supper when he heard familiar voices arguing in a nearby room.

"For God's sake, grow up," said Frank. "You haven't seen him for ages. Just be polite and come down."

"I told you. I don't want to," said Tom. The door slammed, and Frank stormed out, coming face to face with Farcett.

"What's wrong with Tom?" asked Robert. "It was me he was talking about, wasn't it?"

"Yes," said Frank. "But he's not angry about dining with you. He's furious with Montmorency. He wouldn't let Tom go off to Italy with Fregoli. To be honest, I don't really blame Tom for being so cross. Montmorency didn't put up much of a case, and every time Tom explained why he wanted to go, Montmorency just got more stubborn. He let Tom travel with Fregoli in the summer, but now he won't allow him out his sight. He's even started on me the last couple of days – asking me all the time where I'm going, who I'm seeing, when I'll be back. It doesn't make sense. He trusted us more when we were all in danger."

Farcett drew Frank to one side and spoke in a low whisper. "Think about it, Frank. Isn't Montmorency's behaviour entirely natural? He could have lost any one of you in that fire. No wonder he wants to keep you close to him now. And anyway, it seems pretty clear that we may have a wedding on our hands sometime soon. He'd want you both around for that, now wouldn't he?"

"I suppose so," said Frank.

"So why don't you go back and explain that to Tom," said Farcett, "and tell him I'd really appreciate it if he came down to supper. Then, later tonight, perhaps you and I could have a chat about Montmorency. Maybe we can get to the bottom of this strange mood he's in. Trust me, I know about these things. It could be that you are going to be needed here to help pull him out of it."

Frank thought back to Farcett's own brush with despair, and understood that he should do as the doctor said. "OK", he sighed. "I'll try to change Tom's mind."

He half succeeded. Tom joined them at the table, but with a bad grace, and under the weight of his silence, everyone else's conversation was stilted. Montmorency and Frank suggested ways in which Farcett might help the homeless, and Mary told him a little of the history of her home town, but it wasn't the warm welcome the doctor had expected. After the meal, while Montmorency walked Mary home and Tom retreated upstairs, Farcett sat with Frank, alone in the lounge that had throbbed with life before Fregoli left. Frank described how Montmorency had blamed himself for the blaze, and then, after a period of great energy in helping with the reconstruction, had suddenly – in the last couple of days – become gloomy, and obsessed with keeping his family and friends together.

It seemed to Farcett that he might have found his first interesting case-study on the effect of the fire. It fell outside the brief he had been given by Armitage, who was really interested only in the political aftermath of the disaster, but Farcett saw no reason why he shouldn't carry out a wider investigation of his own. After all, Armitage wasn't paying him. What was to stop him doing additional research on the psychological plight of the victims – something that might provide material for a lecture or a published paper, maybe even a book? He would happily send any interesting findings on terrorism straight to Armitage, but he would keep his other observations to himself.

9. WALKING HOME

To anyone looking on, Mary and Montmorency would have seemed a fine couple as they walked arm-in-arm through the dark streets. Her natural grace and tall dignity (and the slightly outmoded dress-sense that was a legacy of her severe mother) made the sixteen-year gap in their ages seem smaller. It was easy to see why she found his dark good looks, almost military bearing, and formal English manners hard to resist. For a while they spoke about arrangements for the next day at the soup kitchen: who would arrive first to light the stove; whether they needed a lock on the shed to stop people stealing vegetables; what they should do about the woman who pretended to be pregnant just to get to the front of the queue. All the time, Montmorency's mind was elsewhere. What if Malpensa had already tracked him down? What if he was here, in Paterson, now – stalking them as they walked, or even back at the hotel, attacking Frank and Tom while he was away with Mary? Should he have told them of the danger, despite Armitage's insistence that he must not? Was he being weak, or strong? He had spent many hours since returning to Paterson trying to remember whether Armitage had insisted that Mary should stay in the town, and he had almost convinced himself that nothing had been said. Wouldn't it be better if she were in a place of safety?

"...don't you think?" He caught the end of a question from Mary, but had no idea what she had asked. She was unsurprised by his distraction. He had been behaving oddly ever since Alex had left. And he still hadn't mentioned the memoir. Had he changed his mind about her? She had thought it was her presence that was keeping him in Paterson. Now it seemed that it was only his urge to make amends for the fire that held him there.

They reached the spot at which Mary had been attacked. Montmorency sensed a new tension in her, and the two of them instinctively looked around for suspicious bystanders, each of them believing that the other was unaware of their fears. All seemed well. But the desire to keep Mary safe was at the front of Montmorency's mind, and he blurted out his thoughts clumsily, taking her by surprise.

"Perhaps you should get away," he said. "Do you have an aunt or someone – maybe somewhere nobody knows about? Somebody you could go and visit?"

Mary stopped walking. "What do you mean? Go away? Why? Would you come too?"

"No. I have to stay..." He wanted to explain, but at that moment a man on the other side of the road stopped, and lit a cigarette. *One of Armitage's agents?* "I'm needed here..."

Mary was suddenly angry, though she tried not to show it. "And I am not?"

"I didn't mean that. It's just..." He couldn't complete the sentence.

"What?"

"It's just that this is no place for you." Montmorency knew he had said the wrong thing before the words had left his lips.

"No place for me! This is my home! I've lived here all my life..."

"I didn't mean…" Across the road, there was a pulse of red light as the man drew on his cigarette. "I just think it might be for the best."

Mary tried not to lose her composure, though she could feel despair seeping through her body as she strode on. What was he saying? Were her prospects of marriage gone? Perhaps he just wanted a little time apart from her to make up his mind. After all, the demands of their relief work meant they had been seeing an awful lot of each other – far more than they might have in 'normal' times. Maybe it wouldn't do any harm to be apart for a while. She had an idea.

"I could take Tom with me, if you like. He wants to get away."

"No!" snapped Montmorency, thrashing around to find a way of explaining without telling her the truth: that if she attached herself to Tom, she would turn herself into a target for Malpensa. "Tom must stay here."

They were outside Mary's gate now.

"I don't understand…" said Mary, in a tone that suggested she did – and that her understanding was that Montmorency no longer loved her.

A woman pushing a baby carriage stopped, apparently rearranging the blankets inside. *An odd time to be out with a child*, Montmorency thought. Was this another of Armitage's spies?

"Please," said Montmorency. "Forget I ever suggested it. I just want to keep you safe."

"Safe from what?" asked Mary. "There are no dangers here that I wouldn't encounter somewhere else."

The woman started wheeling the pram to and fro on the spot – just to arm's length each time, as if soothing the baby with motion, though Montmorency could hear no cries.

Mary continued, "And I think the one thing you should be in no doubt about by now is that I can look after myself!"

He hung his head. "Forgive me. I chose my words badly. I'm exhausted. We both are. Let's talk again tomorrow at the shelter." He reached towards Mary's hand, but she pulled it away, and turned her head out of range of a kiss on the cheek.

"Yes, I will be there," she said, with a formality he had not heard in her voice since they were first introduced.

She closed the gate behind her, and, as the baby carriage was wheeled away, Montmorency watched Mary rummage in her pocket for her key. He couldn't see her tears as she closed the door behind her. Yes, she could look after herself. She was doing a fine job of living alone. But she didn't want to.

As he walked leadenly back to the hotel, Montmorency saw Malpensa behind every tree, and Armitage's men on every corner. He was overwhelmed with the desire to flee – to get back to his house in London and the quiet, leisured life he had worked so hard to achieve. But he knew that, if he left, Malpensa would always be at his heels, and that if he disobeyed Armitage it was not he who would suffer, but Frank, Robert, or Tom. If they weren't hurt physically, they might be socially ruined by what was in the memoir, and he knew that Armitage would have no compunction about using it against them. He was only trying to preserve their lives, in every sense. But it seemed that in doing so he might destroy the love and friendship that were his very reason for living.

10. A LETTER FROM WASHINGTON

Montmorency slept badly, and was in such a serious mood when he woke that the laugher coming from the Breakfast Room seemed almost indecent. Frank and Robert were tucking in when he arrived, and he saw that there was an envelope propped up against the cruet in his usual place at the table. He recognised the handwriting immediately.

"It's from Alex," said Frank. "It seems he's more interested in writing to you than to his own brother. Still, I'm sure you'll read it out to us."

Montmorency picked up the letter, and turned it over. He could see it had been opened and clumsily re-sealed. *Amateurs!* He thought, but then he realised that Armitage wanted him to know that his letters were being intercepted. It was all part of the pressure to make Montmorency comply with his plan.

"What does it say?" Frank nagged. Montmorency knew he could risk reading it aloud. If Alex had revealed anything about Malpensa, the letter would not have been allowed to arrive.

> *My Dear Montmorency,*
> *I do hope you have explained to everyone the reason for my*
> *sudden departure. I write to reassure you that the news from*

Washington is good. Angelina's pregnancy is progressing well. We are assured by the doctors that there is no further cause for alarm. The baby is due to be born in just three months' time. No doubt Robert would think me a fool not to have noticed the signs before. But I am new to this game, which is indeed mysterious, and somewhat daunting, but very exciting.

"You must write back and tell him I'm here," said Doctor Farcett. "And tell him from me that he has no cause to reproach himself. You'd be surprised how little some men know about women's bodies."

Tom was walking in as he spoke, driven to the dining room by hunger, despite his rage and resentment. He could feel himself blushing at the doctor's words. Frank couldn't resist teasing him, even though his own knowledge of the finer points of female anatomy was rather hazy.

"We'd better change the subject," he giggled. "This is hot stuff for Tom."

Tom grabbed some toast. "Why are you all treating me like a child?" he shouted, knocking over the milk jug as he flounced back out of the room.

"Because that's what you are!" Frank yelled back, ignoring Montmorency's silent signal to hold off.

"I'd better go and talk to him," said Montmorency, rising from his seat.

"Don't," said Farcett. "It will only make things worse. Give him a few minutes to calm down first."

They slumped back into casual conversation about how Alexander would measure up to the unexpected demands of fatherhood, unaware of what was going on upstairs.

For Tom had had enough, and was determined to leave, in the hope of catching up with Fregoli before his boat sailed for Naples. He rammed a few clothes into a bag, and went into Montmorency's bedroom to look for money. He had rummaged through five drawers before he found Montmorency's cash box, but as he searched for its key, there was a scraping of chairs from the breakfast room. The others were making for the stairs. Tom froze, groping for an excuse for being in Montmorency's room, but well aware that he had no hope of returning to his own without being spotted. He could hear voices. They were low, almost conspiratorial, but as Montmorency and Farcett settled outside the door Tom could make out what they were saying; and they were talking about him.

"...but you know there's a chance – even a probability – that he'll be left alone here," said Montmorency, believing that Farcett knew all about the threat from Malpensa.

"Come now, old man. Don't speak like that," said Farcett, assuming that after their jokes about the challenges facing Alexander, Montmorency was getting cold feet about marrying Mary, and taking on all the responsibilities of a husband and family man. Maybe he was even wondering whether he was too old for the task.

"Seriously, I'm asking if you'll take the boy on," Montmorency insisted, in a tone that sent Tom into a mix of rage and despair, "and to treat him as if he were your own."

Farcett didn't need reminding of the years he had spent believing that Tom might indeed be his son. "Of course," he said. "Just as if I were his father."

Tom was furious. Montmorency was passing him around like a parcel, or a pet dog that had lost its charm. He frantically continued his search, and found the key to the cash box amongst Montmorency's underwear. Trembling, he managed to open the tin, and pocketed a handful of coins and banknotes. Fearing that the door would open at any moment, he grabbed Montmorency's walking boots, and left the room by the same precarious rooftop route that Montmorency and Alexander had taken at gunpoint five days before.

Farcett was still trying to stiffen Montmorency's resolve: "But you are going to stay here. Promise me that."

"Oh yes," said Montmorency, "Who knows? I could well be here for the rest of my life." *And that may not be very long*, he thought, reaching out for the doorknob.

Frank shouted up from the floor below. "Are you two ready? We're going to be late. We don't want Mary to have to open up on her own."

Montmorency turned away from the door. "Just give me a couple of minutes in the bathroom, and I'll be with you," he yelled. "Is my coat down there?"

"I've got it," said Frank. "And your scarf. Just get a move on!"

Montmorency tapped on Tom's door on the way downstairs. There was no reply. "Don't sulk, Tom," he said, imagining the boy slumped on the bed. "We'll have a proper talk tonight."

Montmorency spent the day working out how to explain to Tom the importance of staying in Paterson without alarming him, or giving away the truth about Malpensa. His distraction only added to Mary's distress. By the time they were clearing up the soup kitchen, he had decided that the best way to calm Tom was to be upbeat, and to paint a positive picture of their new lives together as a family in this land of opportunity and fun. But when Montmorency got back to the hotel that evening and opened his own bedroom door, he realised that Tom was already far away.

11. ON THE ROAD

Tom wasn't sure where he was. He had skirted the main road out of Paterson, keeping hidden amongst the trees, heading east, in what he assumed must be the general direction of New York. He was glad of Montmorency's boots. It was no surprise that they were of the highest quality – Montmorency's weakness for fine clothes was well known – but they were a perfect fit: more evidence, if Tom needed it, that Montmorency was indeed his father. Once clear of the hotel, Tom emptied out his pockets to see what he had gleaned from Montmorency's desk. Alarmed at how much money he had stolen – well over a hundred dollars – he felt a pang of guilt, because he knew the money had been donated to the soup kitchen, to help the victims of the Paterson fire. But wasn't Tom one of those victims? He told himself that if the fire hadn't happened, Montmorency would not have turned into the brooding, unreasonable figure he was today. Fregoli's tour would have swept on from Paterson taking Tom with it: off to the life of greasepaint and laughter where he was happiest. He promised himself that he would pay the money back one day – from the proceeds of his own wonderful show. For now, he would use the cash to speed him on his way to catch up with Fregoli and return to Europe, where his adult life could begin.

But it was cold, and he had no coat. He hadn't planned his getaway at all. Would they be looking for him? Should he disguise himself? Would they have wired ahead to the port at New York, warning the shipping line to look out for him? Maybe he should just hope that he would reach Fregoli in time to borrow a wig before boarding the ship. Or *perhaps*…said a small voice in the back of his mind…perhaps he should return to the hotel, give the money back, and apologise. But Montmorency hadn't seemed in a forgiving mood that morning. He had even been talking about walking out on Tom, and leaving him in Doctor Farcett's care. Tom knew there was only a slim possibility that he would reach New York before Fregoli's ship sailed for Naples, but there must be a chance. Ships had been delayed before. He would carry on.

He heard the sound of a horse and cart coming along the road, and he instinctively hid behind a tree trunk as it passed. When the noise of the hooves had died away, he set off again, stumbling over tree roots as he tried to stay hidden, while using the edge of the road as a guideline for his journey. Within half an hour he was wishing he had waved down the cart and asked for a ride. He was well clear of Paterson now, and surely no stranger would waste their time taking him back there. He could think up an excuse – a sick relative maybe – to explain why he was travelling alone. So he decided to go out in the open, to walk along the smooth surface of the road, and try to stop the very next car, carriage or buggy that passed his way.

It was a long time coming, but when it came, it pulled up of its own accord. He didn't even have to wave.

"Is this the way to the North River?" said a boy, not much older than Tom, as his companion struggled to keep the horse still.

Tom had to think fast. He had never heard of the North River, but this looked like the chance of a ride, and even if the boys weren't going in the right direction for their own purposes, he would be happy to keep travelling east.

"I could show you," he lied, and as the boy who had spoken shuffled sideways to make more room on the bench at the front of the cart, Tom climbed aboard.

The horse plodded on.

"You from round here?" said the boy who had spoken before. "You don't sound like you're from these parts."

Tom tried to put on more of an American accent. "Not really," he said. "Just passing through."

"They call me Pop," said the boy who was holding the reins. "And that next to you is Billy."

From the tone of Pop's voice, Tom knew that the he should give his own name, but what should it be? Tom, or something made up? He thought it unlikely that these boys would be checking up on him, and if this was going to be a long journey, he would have enough lies to keep track of without having to remember a fake name.

"I'm Tom," he said. "Good to meet you." And then, to put off the moment when they asked more questions, he added, "What takes you to the North River?"

"We're going to get jobs on the ice harvest," mumbled Billy.

"The what?" said Tom. "Did you say you were starving?"

Pop said it more slowly. "Ice harvest. You cut blocks of ice out of the frozen lakes, and they store them up to sell in Manhattan in the summer."

Tom was glad to hear mention of Manhattan. "That's where I'm going," he said.

Billy brightened, "To the ice harvest?"

"No, to Manhattan. I have to catch a ship."

Pop took his eyes off the road and looked at Tom more closely. "What ship? Where to?"

Tom paused for a moment too long.

"You're running away, aren't you?" said Pop.

Tom could tell he must be looking shifty, but Billy laughed. "It takes one to know one!" he said.

"So you're…"

"Yes," said Pop. "We're running away too. Running away from the silk factory in Paterson. You been there?"

"Not inside," said Tom. "But I know it."

"Then you'll have heard what it's like in there," said Pop. "The noise, the danger. Being treated like dirt. And it's even worse since the fire…"

"You heard about the fire?" said Billy.

"Oh yes," said Tom, not wanting to reveal that he had been at the heart of the conflagration. "I heard about that."

Billy carried on: "There's nothing left for guys like us in Paterson now. My folks expect me to work all day and spend the night in a tent with all the kids screaming and puking all over the place. It'll be years before they get the house built back up, and by then the factory will be closed and there'll be no jobs."

"But why would the factory close?"

"Well," said Pop, "For one, there's a rumour that old man Bayfield is going to run out of money, paying out on the insurance policies people took out before the fire…"

"And for two," said Billy, "the workers themselves are going to bring it down. There's going to be trouble real soon. A strike."

"But that might get you more money, better conditions," said Tom.

"Maybe one day," said Pop. "But for now a strike just means no pay, and up at the ice harvest they pay well."

Tom was labouring to stay in the conversation without giving away his connections with Paterson. "I've got friends who worked in an ice cream factory in London," he said, thinking back to stories Montmorency and Frank had told about their time undercover on the trail of terrorists. "They said it was horrible. And you should hear what they put in the ice cream. Wood shavings, coloured dye…"

"This is ice, not ice cream," said Pop, with a note of contempt in his voice. "It's hard work. Men's work." He was looking at Tom's soft white hands.

Tom was all too aware that, since leaving Tarimond, his only jobs had been sorting out Fregoli's costumes and a bit of potato peeling at the soup kitchen.

"I'm not afraid of work," he said.

They rolled on in silence for a few minutes. The quiet was broken by an unmistakable bubbling noise from Pop's trousers.

Billy laughed. "That's why we call him Pop," he said.

"I can't help it," said Pop. "It's the way I'm made."

"Just as well you're going for outdoor work," said Tom.

"You should join us," said Billy. "What's so special about this ship of yours? You looking for work there, or going some place else?"

"I've got people to meet," said Tom, trying to keep things vague. "In any case, I'm not sure I'd manage in the cold, hacking away at a frozen lake. If I reach that ship at New York in time, I'll be off to Italy for sunshine, laughter, and fabulous food."

"Yeah, we've heard all that from the Italians in the silkworks. It won't be like that you know. If Italy's so wonderful, why have they all come here?"

"No, it is. My friends have been there. Those people from the ice cream factory…"

Billy rolled his eyes at Pop. London, Italy, ice cream. It was clear they thought Tom was some kind of fantasist, with a new story to match every occasion.

Pop pulled on the reins. "I'm hungry," he said. "Let's stop for a while. You got any food in that bag of yours?"

For the past two hours Tom had been regretting his failure to stock up before he left. "Nothing," he said.

"Well, don't go thinking we're going to feed you," said Billy. "We've hardly got enough for the two of us."

They all got down from the cart. Pop released the horse from the traces and led it to a brook, where it gulped the water, eagerly. Then he tied it to a tree by its reins, and sat down to split a loaf and some cheese between Billy and himself while Billy built a rudimentary fire.

Tom stood apart, watching, hunger gnawing at his stomach. "I could pay you. I could buy some food," he said.

"Yeah, right," said Pop. "Like you've got no food, and no job, but you've got money."

"Yes, I have," said Tom, reaching into his pocket and pulling out a banknote at random. It was a five-dollar bill.

Pop and Billy stared at it. "Where did you get that? You stole it?"

"No," said Tom. "It's from my friend... my father. The one I told you about..."

Pop sneered. "Oh yeah, in London. Or was it Italy? And he's your Dad now. Give me a break."

"No please, believe me. I can explain," said Tom, pulling more money from his pocket in the hope that it would convince them of his goodwill. He was spared their bemused contempt when the horse suddenly neighed, bucked, and pulled its rein so tight that the rotten branch to which Pop had tied it split in two. The beast ran off across the brook into a clump of trees.

"Don't worry. I'll get him back," Tom shouted, stuffing the money into Billy's palm and splashing across the water. Pop and Billy watched in astonishment as Tom pursued the horse through the trees, across a field, and cornered it by a fence. They couldn't hear what he was saying as he closed in, gingerly, finally giving the beast a reassuring pat as he took hold of its bridle and gently coaxed it back towards the campfire.

"Where did you learn to do that?" asked Pop, as Tom tied the horse up, more securely this time, to a sturdy tree trunk, "I had you down as a town boy."

"At home. On Tarimond, where I grew up," said Tom, gradually getting his breath back. "I was with horses all the time there."

"Tarimond? Where's that?"

"It ain't round here, I can tell you," said Billy.

"Scotland. It's an island. Off the west coast."

"Scotland?" Said Pop, fingering the banknotes Billy had passed to him. "Scotland, London, Italy..."

"Believe me. I know it sounds a bit far-fetched, but it's all true," said Tom, realising from Pop's contemptuous shrug that that he was only making himself sound more of a liar.

"We don't want to get tied up with no criminal," said Billy. "We've got enough trouble without getting on the wrong side of the law."

"Please," said Tom. "Please, believe me, the money isn't stolen. It's only borrowed. I'll pay it back one day. Montmorency knows that."

"Montmorency? Who's he? The Ice Cream Man?"

"Yes...no...my father. Well, I think so now..."

"And he's where? Scotland, London, Italy, Timbuktu?"

Just in time, Tom stopped himself saying that Montmorency was in Paterson. He realised that Pop and Billy might guess he was one of the Europeans so well known for helping after the fire.

"I'm hoping I'll meet him on that ship," he said, inwardly congratulating himself on coming up with a lie that didn't require a whole new story to back it up. He was desperate to change the subject. "Look," he said, as Pop and Billy stared at him. "I've got money. You've got food. Thanks to me, you've got your horse back. I reckon the three of us can get along as far as the North River, don't you?"

Pop put the money in his pocket and handed over a corner of bread and a lump of cheese. "I guess so," he said, "and it seems like you'll be keeping us entertained with some stories along the way."

12. THE COVER UP

Montmorency was lying on his bed, staring at the ceiling, trying to decide what to do. He had dug out his favourite old opera hat from his luggage, and pushed its collapsible crown up and down as he thought things through. *Thwhopp*, it went, as he tested one idea. *Thwhopp*, as he tried another. Years before, he had lain on anther bed, in another hotel, weighing up the pros and cons of his plan to lead a double life. Until now, it had seemed that the gamble had paid off: his daring had been rewarded with two decades of prosperity, friendship and adventure. But ultimately it had led to the mess he was in today: his son lost, his own life under threat, and all his friends in peril unless he lied to them.

He ran through his options. He could go after Tom, but that would risk drawing attention to himself, and endangering all those left behind in Paterson: putting them at the mercy of Armitage's agents and Malpensa too. He could leave Tom to his own devices, but he was a young man facing unknown dangers in a strange land. Those risks were bad enough, but Tom was unaware that Malpensa was alive, that he might well be in the area, and that he probably knew – from the newspaper reports – that Tom was Montmorency's son. Tom knew nothing of Armitage, who had made it perfectly clear that he would sacrifice any or all of Montmorency's family and friends in his bid to capture Malpensa. If Armitage discovered that Tom was away from Paterson, possibly luring Malpensa away from his trap, he would have no compunction about removing the boy from the equation. Surely, as a father, Montmorency should try to find Tom and bring him back to Paterson?

But...*thwhopp*.

But...*thwhopp*.

But there was always a chance that Tom would catch up with Fregoli. After all, he had plenty of money with him. He might reach the ship in time, or get himself a ticket for another, not far behind. If Tom could only get on board an ocean liner, he would be safe for at least a week, whatever horrors awaited the rest of them in Paterson. And who knew, in a week's time, maybe all this drama would be over. However events played out, whether Montmorency lived or died, Tom was likely to be safer in Europe, and – if Armitage's plan to capture or kill Malpensa worked out – safe for good.

But how could Tom's absence be covered up? Not just from Frank, Robert and Mary, but from the hotel staff, any number of whom might be in the pay of Armitage.

Thwhopp. Again, Montmorency's mind jumped back twenty years; to the time at the Marimion hotel when he had played the part of the wealthy guest, Montmorency, and his rough servant, Scarper. It had worked then. And here it would be easier, because Tom's stubborn sulkiness had laid the foundations for the trick.

Everyone thought Tom was in his own room now, refusing to come down for food, or even to answer the door. If Montmorency were to take Tom's meals up to him, while passing on Tom's insistence that he should not be disturbed, no one need know that he had run away. Indeed, if Montmorency could sustain the arguments with Frank about the unfairness of Tom being kept in Paterson, the chances were that Armitage's spies in the hotel would report the rows back, and Armitage would have no reason to think that Tom was on the loose.

Montmorency was sure he could keep the deception going long enough to let Tom get well clear of Paterson. He slipped into Tom's room and stuffed cushions and clothes under the sheets, so that if anybody caught a glimpse through the doorway, it would look as if Tom was in the bed. But as he was taking the key from the door, so he could lock the room from the outside, he heard footsteps on the landing.

It was Doctor Farcett. He knocked gently on Tom's door. "Tom, Tom," he said. "Tom, do come down."

Montmorency put his arm across his mouth to muffle the sound of his voice. "Go away," he said, trying to imitate Tom.

"No, Tom, let me in," said the doctor, and for a moment Montmorency contemplated opening the door and explaining his new plan. But the doorknob began to turn, and Montmorency instinctively leant against the door to keep Farcett out. It would be simpler not to compromise Robert by giving him yet another secret to carry. He was doing remarkably well hiding those Armitage had piled upon him, but there must come a point where his mental equilibrium would be upset by the strain. Best for him to be kept in the dark about Tom.

The doctor stopped pushing on the door. "OK, Tom," he said. "Have it your way. But you must understand – your father has his reasons for keeping you here. I can assure you they are very good reasons, and that you will both be happier if you stay. Now please, don't shut yourself away."

Montmorency grunted a reply, but it was drowned out by the voice of a chambermaid. "Is everything all right, sir?"

Montmorency sensed that his plan was about to be upset. The woman would come into the room while he was still there, and guess that the body in the bed was a fake. He started composing an excuse for being in Tom's room, alone, but he was rescued by Farcett's reply to the maid.

"No, no. All's well. Master Tom is just rather overtired. I think it would be best if we all left him undisturbed for a while. There's no need for you to tidy his room. Just give him time to recover. I'll keep an eye on him. I have some medicine in my bag that will probably do the trick if he needs it. Let's leave him in peace for now."

"Of course, Doctor," said the girl, and Montmorency heard the two of them set off down the stairs.

Once again, Robert Farcett had astounded Montmorency with his calm response to danger. Clearly he had guessed the situation and seen the need to head off the maid. He probably assumed that she was one of Armitage's spies. Montmorency waited till he was sure the corridor was empty again, then he quietly left Tom's room, locked the door and went down to the smoking room, where the doctor was warming himself at the fire, alone.

Farcett spoke first. "I'm worried about Tom," he said.

"Me too," said Montmorency. "I think we should give him some time to cool off. I will take his supper to his room tonight. It's going to be hard for him to re-emerge after making such a spectacle of himself before."

"Good idea," said Doctor Farcett. "I'll ask the staff to leave him alone for a day or so, until he's feeling better."

With his back to the door, Montmorency had not noticed a waiter arriving with a decanter of sherry. Until he was offered a drink, he'd had no idea the man was in the room, or how long he had been able to hear the conversation. Yet again, Montmorency mentally congratulated the doctor on managing to indicate to him that he understood the gravity of their plight without giving the slightest hint to outsiders.

As the servant turned to go, Farcett calmly said to him, "Please tell the kitchen to put Master Tom's dinner on a tray. Mr Montmorency will take it up to him." There was no guilt or deception in Robert's voice. Montmorency couldn't know the reason: the doctor was completely unaware of the dangers swirling around them.

13. THE DOCTOR GETS BUSY

In the morning, Montmorency made a bit of a pantomime of failing to rouse Tom from his bed, which successfully stirred Frank to have another go at him for keeping Tom in Paterson. Montmorency let their row go on for long enough for the staff to notice, and then asked for a tray, so that he could take Tom's breakfast upstairs. He let himself in to Tom's room, ate the food, and made his way back down, wedging a small piece of paper in the door as he locked it, so that he would be able to tell later whether anyone had gone inside. By now Mary had arrived and, in one corner of the breakfast room, was in earnest conversation with Doctor Farcett. He was unpacking a trunk that had been sent on from the hospital in Buffalo. It was full of medical equipment: jars of pills, bottles of linctus and lotion, syringes, bandages, and strange hooks, probes and tubes that looked more suited for work on the drains than for sorting out human problems. *Armitage got that lot here quickly*, thought Montmorency, glad that Frank didn't seem at all suspicious that Farcett's luggage had arrived so soon.

"I'd like to come to the soup kitchen today," said the doctor. "It might be the best place for me to set up my little clinic."

Montmorency was pleased. "Yes, whether anyone wants your medical attention or not, we could do with an extra pair of hands. It looks as if Tom won't be joining us today."

"Oh dear," said Mary. "I feel terribly guilty about causing all this trouble between you."

Montmorency took an instant to register that she was, understandably, assuming that he was keeping Tom in town because of their impending marriage. The moment of mystification on his face was enough to unsettle Mary. Farcett dived in to break the awkward silence.

"Oh it's not your fault at all," he said.

"No, nothing to do with you," added Montmorency, too late, and in a tone that lacked any of the fondness he ached with.

They talked for a while about the practical arrangements for incorporating Robert's medical centre into the soup kitchen.

Frank interrupted, asking Montmorency, "Aren't you hungry?"

"What?"

"You haven't had any breakfast."

Montmorency realised that he must work harder at the details of his subterfuge. He buttered a piece of cold toast he really didn't fancy, having eaten everything on Tom's tray ten minutes before.

"We can't have you falling ill," said the doctor, jokily swinging his stethoscope.

Mary spoke up. "I've noticed that you've not been yourself these last few days."

Montmorency couldn't help snapping back. "There's nothing wrong with me. I'm just a bit tired, that's all. Now, let's get off. And Mary, perhaps when we're finished at the soup kitchen, you could give Robert a good tour of the town."

He had meant it to sound like a gesture of his confidence in her – an acknowledgement of her familiarity with Paterson, its population and their many needs. To Mary's ears it was another incidence of him wanting to get her out of his way.

They left for the soup kitchen in silence.

14. ONWARDS TO THE ICE

While a bundle of pillows and clothes slumbered in his bed at the Patterson hotel, Tom spent the night in the cold, under canvas. He had helped Billy string up a makeshift tent using a tarpaulin from the back of the cart, and then he had built a campfire, which he lit without the benefit of matches. Pop was amazed at how this strange foreigner, with his stories of life in the great cities of the world, was so well endowed with country skills, but he was grateful that the horse was securely tied for the night, and that a rabbit caught by Tom was roasting tastily over the flames.

They talked more about the ice field on the North River, and Tom started retelling stories he'd heard from Frank and Montmorency about the ice cream factory. He played all the parts: the fearsome manager, the filthy manageress, the coy (and not-so-coy) women on the factory floor – literally so when a dispute turned into a riot, with churns of cream spilt underfoot.

Pop and Billy laughed. "You should be on the stage!" said Pop.

"It left three hours ago," said Billy, completing the old joke.

"I was," said Tom.

"What?"

"I was. On the stage. Or at least I used to help backstage…"

"Yeah, yeah," said Pop, with undisguised disbelief, and Tom realised that they would never believe him if he started on about his time touring with Fregoli.

"You're a funny one," said Pop, "and, of course not much more than a hundred years ago, you'd have been the enemy. The one thing I do believe about you is that you're English."

"Scottish, actually," said Tom, his voice trailing off as he added, "though I suppose my parents are English."

"Scottish, English, it's all the same," said Billy. "We beat you in the revolution. That's why we have our President, and not your Queen."

"King," said Tom. "She died in January. We've got Edward the Seventh now."

"Well I never," said Pop. "How did I miss that? Still, we've had a busy time here, what with the assassination and all."

"Montmorency was there," Tom blurted out. His voice trailed away as he added, "When President McKinley was shot." He knew this would be the last straw for his new friends.

Pop rolled his eyes and yawned. "That was before your friend went to the moon, I suppose?"

Tom forced a smile, and pulled his jacket tight against the wind. It was cold, and they snuggled up close in the tent. They were all tired, and they slept well, with Pop popping away fragrantly from time to time in his dreams.

In the morning, Tom – wanting to make himself useful so that they would not abandon him in the wild – fed and watered the horse, and attached it carefully to the cart. As the sun rose ahead of them, they continued along the road, confident that they must be going east, but with no idea where they were until, at last, they came to a fork in the road, with a signpost pointing to a place called Fort Lee.

"Now there's a place you'll have heard of," said Pop.

"I'm sorry?" said Tom.

"Surely you've heard of Fort Lee? They told us about it at school. It was important in the revolution. I can't remember why, exactly."

"It's from when you Brits were winning," said Billy, not realising that Pop had stopped himself from admitting that they weren't at one of America's most glorious historic sites.

"Yeah, but we won in the end, didn't we?" said Pop. "Anyway, what they taught us was that General Washington built Fort Lee to guard the way to New York."

"So we're near New York?" said Tom, excited that he might get a chance to break away and try to find Fregoli.

"Looks like it. And that means we can't be far from the North River, either," said Pop.

"So we'll take the road to Fort Lee?"

"Might as well. There's nothing to tell us where the other track goes, and if somewhere's signposted, you can be pretty sure there'll be people, and where there's people we can find someone who can show us the way to the North River."

So they took the right fork in the road, with hope in their hearts.

15. MARY AND THE DOCTOR

With a wobbly table and some makeshift screens, Doctor Farcett set up a consulting area at the back of the soup kitchen tent. His mind was mainly on the task that interested him most: assessing the psychological impact of the fire on the citizens of Paterson. But he had half an ear to their political views, ready to note for Armitage any signs of radicalism and dissent. Nevertheless, most of what his patients had to say seemed unremarkable. They were mothers concerned about their children's spots or sniffles, or about the next member of their growing families, and already on the way.

At lunchtime, Frank came over with a bowl of soup. "Here, have some of this. You've earned it. You've been busier than I expected. I'm not going to catch anything coming over here, am I?"

"Thanks," said Farcett, putting the bowl on the table to cool. "I always find you get a good turn-out for medical advice when it's free. It makes me wonder what's lurking out there amongst people who think they've got better things to spend their money on than seeing to a cough or a rash."

"Is that what you've been seeing today? Coughs and rashes?"

"Well, it's not so much what I've seen, as what I've been hearing about. A lot of people seem to have friends or relatives with breathing problems, or itchy hands. I wonder if I've arrived at the start of an epidemic."

"I don't think it's anything infectious," said Frank.

"Well, thank you, Doctor Fox-Selwyn," said Robert – his sarcasm falling just on the right side of giving offence – "I'll throw away my medical text books and defer to you in future."

Frank let the implied criticism go. "Did it occur to you why the people with the coughs and rashes didn't come to see you themselves?" he asked.

"I imagine they were at work," said Farcett. "And anyway, I've only started here today. If you ask me, it's remarkable how many people did turn up."

"Exactly," said Frank. "They couldn't leave their jobs. Lots of people in the silk factory are sick. I saw it myself when I worked there a few years back. It's the dust in the air from the fibres. It can get right down into your chest. And I wouldn't like to be up to my elbows in some of the dyes they use in there."

"Maybe I should set up in the factory then?" said Farcett, not really meaning what he said. But Frank took him seriously.

"Too right. And not just to listen to wheezing chests and soothe itchy hands. You say you're interested in the way the fire has affected people here – how it's tipped their mental balance. Well, if you ask me working in that factory has a bigger effect on people's minds than one night of blazing terror – even if they lost their homes. That can be put right. A lifetime of slaving away in the silkworks is enough to consign any sane man or woman to a pit of despair. I've lived among them, remember. I've seen it."

Farcett was interested, and saw straight away that the factory might not only be clinically rewarding, but that it could be the best place to look for the political unrest that interested Armitage.

"I see what you mean. Do you think they'd let me set up shop in there? Could you get me in?"

"I can't go back inside," said Frank.

"It's that bad?"

"No, it's not that – or not just that, anyway. I know I look and sound a bit different from how I was when I worked there, and that probably explains why no one seems to have recognised me, but if I were to go back in – in that context, even with a different name, someone might put two and two together."

"And?"

"Well, I know the government thinks all the firebrands have been cleared out of Paterson, but can we really be certain? Someone might be left. Somebody who suspects – or even knows – that 'Volpe' didn't really die in that shoot-out in London. Someone who will realise I was that man."

Farcett looked around to make sure no one was in earshot. "Do you think there's real radicalism in there?" he whispered.

"I don't know, but all the ingredients are in place: poor conditions, low pay, bad management, bullying. What more do you need?"

Mary walked towards them. "What are you two cooking up?" she asked.

Frank forced a smile as Farcett started drinking his soup. "Robert was just filling me in on the health of our citizens," said Frank.

"Without giving away any secrets, of course," said Robert.

"*Our citizens*," said Mary. "I'm glad to hear you use that phrase, Frank. Does that mean you feel at home here now?"

Robert interrupted before Frank could reply. "Frank thinks that if I want to see how sick or well people really are, I should examine the workers at the factory."

"He's probably right," said Mary. "Especially these days. I wouldn't mind getting a look in there myself. Would you like me to come with you?"

"That would be wonderful," said Robert. "They might not object to a foreign doctor muscling in if he's accompanied by a local. A charming local, should I say?"

Mary ignored the compliment. "We'd need the owner's permission, first. The place belongs to a man called Harrison Bayfield. He lives in the big house on the hill. He's an insurance man himself – inherited the silk business from his brother."

"I've met him, actually," said Farcett, "though I doubt whether he'll remember me. It was on the ship across from England, the first time I came. That would be about '98, I think. What a lot has happened since then."

Mary looked around the tent, a symbol of the crisis in so many lives. "What a lot, indeed," she said. "And there are people who need our help waiting outside." She took Farcett's empty bowl. "Back to work, gentlemen. And when we're done this afternoon, Robert, why don't we start our tour of Paterson with a walk up the hill to see whether Harrison Bayfield is at home?"

"That would be delightful," said Robert, who was already formulating the structure of his industrial study in his mind. The afternoon passed slowly for him. He couldn't wait to get his new project underway.

While Mary and the doctor walked up past the waterfall to Harrison Bayfield's grand house, Montmorency and Frank made their way in the other direction – back to the hotel. Montmorency could feel that they were being watched, but whether by Armitage's men or by Malpensa himself, he couldn't say. He ached to tell

Frank why he was so miserable, so preoccupied; but he knew that if Frank found out about the danger surrounding them, his response would be to lash out, and to make things even worse. At least Frank seemed to appreciate that this was not the time to revisit Montmorency's treatment of Tom.

It was only late afternoon, but the wintery daylight had almost gone. Frank suggested a drink in the smoking room before they went to freshen up for supper.

"I'll just go and check on Tom," said Montmorency.

The scrap of paper he had set in Tom's doorframe that morning was still in place, but while half of Montmorency's brain rejoiced that no one had entered the room, the other half reminded him that Armitage's spies were professionals, and would have had the sense to reposition it if it had fallen out. The bogus figure was still in the bed. Montmorency gave it a loving pat, and gently redistributed books and clothes, just in case anyone else was keeping an eye on the room.

When he got downstairs again, Frank was snoozing in an armchair, with a newspaper open across his chest. The front page had an account of Fregoli's arrival in New York, with pictures of the great entertainer and his troupe smiling and waving on the steps of a grand hotel. Montmorency had no doubt that Armitage had arranged the photographs, and the captions, which just happened to mention that Fregoli had left his British friends (their names all listed) back in Paterson, New Jersey. Montmorency knew that Armitage would have made sure the story was in all the New York papers, and possibly many others, to maximise the chance of Malpensa seeing it. If he had, Montmorency was a dead man.

16. THE MIGHTY

FALLEN

As soon as Mary and Robert entered the grounds of the big house, they knew that Harrison Bayfield was in trouble. The driveway up to the majestic front steps had not been swept, and in a large urn by the front door the straggly winter corpse of a lavender bush barely hid assorted cigarette ends and cigar butts, no doubt discarded by Bayfield as he stood on the terrace, surveying the remains of his business empire.

They rang the doorbell, expecting the butler to greet them, but it was Harrison Bayfield himself who – after their third ring – opened the door, and then only wide enough to tell them to leave him alone.

Mary, shocked at the dead eyes and stubbled chin she could see through the crack, spoke gently: "Please, Mr Bayfield, it's Mary Gibson. I've brought Doctor Farcett to see you."

"No doctor can help me," said Bayfield, closing the door, but stopping himself when he saw he risked crushing Mary's hand, in its tiny white glove.

"He's not here to treat you," said Mary. "He wants to help the people of Paterson. Please let us in, and we can explain."

Bayfield let out a cynical guffaw: "Help the people of Paterson! I suppose you want money. Let me tell you, the people of Paterson are bankrupting me. You're knocking on the wrong door."

"We don't want money," said Mary. "We just want you to let us into your factory. Maybe it would be easier if we could talk about this inside."

"My brother's factory, you mean," said Bayfield, letting the door open a little wider. "I never wanted to get into the silk game, though at least it still brings in a bit of cash. I'm an insurance man. Or was, I should say. It's remarkable how quickly the vultures start to circle." He fumbled with the lock. "You might as well come in."

Mary and Robert stepped in to the hall. With its oriental rugs, marble staircase and ornate chandelier, it was still impressive, though Robert could tell from a mark on the wallpaper that a large picture was missing.

Bayfield saw Mary drag the tip of her finger along the dusty surface of the hall table. "I've had to let the staff go," he said. "There's just Cook now. She's got no family, so she's offered to stay on in exchange for shelter, but she's too old for housework, and she has her pride."

"Forgive me," said Mary, appalled at her lapse of good manners, "We haven't come here to gloat."

"I wouldn't blame you if you had," said Bayfield, ushering them in to the drawing room, and examining a row of decanters for a trickle of whisky to offer Doctor Farcett. "Take a good look round. I'm sure all your friends would like to know that I'll have to sell all this stuff off. My humiliation won't be complete without a good dose of local gossip."

"Nothing for me," said Farcett, as Bayfield started filling a dirty tumbler. "And I can assure you that Mary and I have no intention of passing on any information about your circumstances. I take it that your insurance business has been badly hit by the fire."

"Not 'badly hit'. Destroyed. I held all the big policies in this town. How could I ever have expected everyone to claim at once – and just when I had taken out a huge loan to modernise the house? The bankers aren't stupid: they want their money back. The builders are smart, too. I've paid them for the materials, and they're using my bricks on repair jobs all over town. They've left me with a hole in the back wall, and only a sheet of canvas between me and the winter. They know I can't afford a lawyer to fight them. Not unless I can muster the energy to sell all this." He waved his arm to take in the grand furniture chosen by Curtis and Cissie, his late brother and his wife, in the early 1890s. "It's all out of style now. It'll raise a fraction of its original value. And who else would want a house like this? Anyone rich enough to buy it could build their own – up to date, and in a town that hasn't just been burnt to the ground." He swigged at the drink he had poured out for Farcett. "I was doing fine till Curtis died, and left me this white elephant, and that wretched factory. I used the works as collateral against the loan. That will be gone too, if the banks close in."

"It's the factory we'd like to talk about, sir," said Robert, awkwardly conscious that he had not properly introduced himself. He held out his hand, "Robert Farcett. We met some years ago, crossing the Atlantic. You brought me here with my friend Montmorency to meet your brother. I doubt you remember…"

Bayfield shrugged. "It seems like another age, doesn't it?" he said, looking into the middle distance. "Mary, you used to come here with your mother, didn't you? Remember all those grand dinners? How is your mother?"

"She passed away, sir, a while back, before your brother's death. I live on my own now."

"But not for long, I'm sure – a charming girl like you. Perhaps you and Doctor Farcett…"

Mary blushed, and Farcett jumped in, "No, no, I assure you. Miss Gibson is merely helping me with my work here – which is why we have come to see you."

"And what has your work to do with me?"

"I came to Paterson to see whether I could assist with the medical needs of the townsfolk after the fire," said Robert. "I've realised that many of them work in your factory, and I wonder whether I might be allowed to set up a small consulting room there, to see how the health of your workforce has been affected." He knew that if he told the full truth – that he wanted to assess the toll taken by the working conditions and to look out for political dissent – he might only make Bayfield imagine a new torrent of catastrophes: expensive reforms, industrial unrest, and strikes. So he tried to find a way to make the project attractive to Bayfield. "After all, a healthy workforce must be the key to good output, and a better profit."

Bayfield sneered: "Profit. Now there's a word I haven't heard for a while."

Mary ignored his tone, and picked up on Doctor Farcett's sentiment, "Perhaps everyone could benefit from Robert's work. The people might be healthier and happier, and your financial troubles might be lessened."

"What the heck," said Bayfield, wearily – quickly remembering he was in the presence of a lady. "Excuse my language, ma'am. You go ahead with your little project. I'll write a note telling the works manager to make available whatever facilities you need."

"I'm sure you won't regret it," said Farcett, brightly.

Bayfield shook his head, "I've plenty of other things to regret. I doubt I'll be around long enough to know whether your study is a good or bad idea."

Both Robert and Mary were too polite to ask him what he meant, though they both feared that he was hinting at suicide. They waited while he scribbled the letter, and left, with awkward goodbyes.

On the walk down the hill, Robert told Mary how concerned he was about Harrison Bayfield's mental health. "He really shouldn't be left alone up there. I'm worried he'll do something stupid."

"Did you see all those empty bottles?" said Mary. "I think he's been drinking – and I don't think he's been enjoying it." She looked out across the town below them. "Imagine. Everyone down there envies him. Even I have been angry with him for not donating much to the rebuilding work. If only they knew."

"But they mustn't," said Farcett. "He probably wouldn't have told us so much about his financial affairs if he had been completely sober. Spreading rumours will only make his creditors close in sooner." But Farcett's mind wasn't only on Bayfield's immediate welfare. Details of the tycoon's mental deterioration might greatly enhance his study of the effects of the fire – showing how it had hit all social classes in the town. He took Mary's arm to help her over a puddle. "I think we should revisit him as soon as possible. Maybe you could go once we've set up at the factory tomorrow? Perhaps you could talk him into letting me examine him?"

"I agree. He shouldn't be by himself," said Mary. "I've enjoyed his family's hospitality plenty of times over the years. It's only right that I should give something back, even if it's only a few hours of friendly conversation."

17. FORT LEE

Billy and Pop were standing at the cliff edge in Fort Lee, imagining George Washington at the same spot in 1776, as British ships were unsuccessfully attacked in the narrow stretch of water separating the mainland from Manhattan. Tom was pretending to do the same, but his mind was on the opposite shore, wondering how he could get across to find Fregoli before he left for Europe.

Suddenly, he had a feeling he was being watched. As he turned, a deep male voice boomed out.

"These are the times that try men's souls."

Pop and Billy looked round too, to see a tall man with a strange machine – some sort of box with a handle, supported by three spindly legs.

The man raised his cap. "Davy Sprocket, at your service."

Tom laughed, "Very good. Just the right name for a camera man!"

"What?" said Pop.

"Sprocket," said Tom. "It's a joke about film. Davy Crockett – Davy Sprocket. Get it?"

"No," said Billy. "What are you talking about?"

The man with the box walked closer. "He's right," he said. "It's good to have found someone who understands my professional name. I'm thinking of changing it. I've got a feeling I've been too clever by half."

"He's talking about the film in his camera," said Tom. "It's held in place by sprocket holes."

"What camera?" said Billy. "What film?"

Tom sighed. "That contraption is a camera. It's for making moving pictures. You must have seen them."

"Sure I have," said Billy, unconvincingly.

"Well, this gentleman here's making a film, if you ask me." Tom took a look at the camera. "It's an Edison. The film is secured on sprocket holes and driven past the lens when you turn the handle."

"Yeah, yeah," said Pop. "Where'd you learn that? London, Scotland, Italy?"

"In Paris, actually," said Tom. "With Fregoli." He stopped himself as he realised his companions would think he was fantasising again.

The man came closer. "Did you say Fregoli?"

"Yes, sir, I worked with him, sir."

Pop interrupted, "You don't want to believe everything he says, Mr Sprocket. He's just a country boy. He can catch a rabbit and tame a horse."

"But it seems he knows about cameras, too," said Davy Sprocket. "Show me what you know, boy."

Tom hesitated, not sure whether he should be talking to a stranger, but he wanted to show Pop that he wasn't lying. "Well, sir. Have you come here to film the battle site? If you have, you'll need to make sure you've got your back to the light. If I were you, I'd stand just where we were standing, and point the lens over there. How much film have you got?"

"It's a new reel."

"Then it will last about two minutes. I'd wait till a boat comes by, or some people to walk along the cliff, otherwise it won't be a very interesting shot."

"Shot?" gasped Billy.

"It's what they call taking a moving picture," said Tom. "There are no guns involved. Then the film has to be developed, and after that it can be projected on a screen, so you can see what you've got – though you can get a rough idea by holding it up to the light, of course."

"I knew all that," said Pop.

"He's right," said Davy Sprocket. "If you boys will lend me a hand, and maybe walk around a bit in front of the camera when I tell you, I'll buy you a drink when we're finished."

Pop and Billy were too keen on the idea of a free drink to argue, and Tom wanted to show off his film-making skills, so they helped carry the tripod to the cliff edge, with Tom jabbering on about focus and processing, in an attempt to impress them all. Then they took it in turns to walk along the cliff-top and pretend to look across to Manhattan. Tom, who had done it before for Fregoli, knew how important it was not to look straight at the camera. Pop and Billy couldn't take their eyes off it. Afterwards, Davy lived up to his promise, and took them for a beer at his hotel.

"Thank you, Mr Sprocket," said Tom.

"I think we can drop the Sprocket thing now. The joke's wearing a bit thin, and it only works on people who've heard of Davy Crockett, anyway."

"Who's Davy Crockett?" said Billy.

"That's settled then," said Davy. "It's back to Davy Payne."

"Like Tom Paine?" said Pop, adding, "These are the times that try men's souls."

"Now I don't know what you're talking about," said Tom.

Pop was glad to have the chance to show off at last. "It's a quotation, from the War of Independence. Tom Paine said it just after Washington had to retreat from here."

"Quite right," said Davy. "That's why I wanted to work here. As far as I know, Tom Paine was no relation of mine. He doesn't even spell his name the same way. But I can't help admiring him, with all he said about freedom and the rights of man. I'm thinking of making a longer film, or lots of films shown one after the other, telling the story of our fight for independence. What do you think?"

"Sounds like a good idea," said Tom.

"Of course, I'll need actors. That's what got me interested in you three. You look as if you'd make good soldiers. It's why I got you to parade around in front of the camera just now."

"He'd have to play a Brit," said Billy. "That's what he is, really."

Tom had been using his American accent, but he dropped it now. "That's right," he said. "But I wouldn't mind for this battle – we won. Just so long as I don't end up dead at the end of the film!"

"No one will hear what any of you say, anyway, so you could be from Australia and it wouldn't matter," said Davy.

"He'll probably tell us he's been there, too," said Pop.

They all looked at Tom, fully prepared for an outrageous tale of derring-do in the Outback. "No, I haven't," said Tom, relieved that, at last, he could seem just a little bit normal.

Davy Payne ordered another round of drinks, and rummaged in his bag for the money to pay. He took out a newspaper and dumped it on the table. The front page story brought a gasp from Tom. It showed Fregoli and his entourage waving from the deck of a departing ship. Tom seized the paper, and stared at the photograph.

The caption confirmed that the great Italian impressionist was already at sea on his way back to Europe. The tears in Tom's eyes stopped him reading the rest of the article – carefully placed there by Armitage – which reprised the story of the Paterson fire and gave full details of the whereabouts of Montmorency.

"So you really did know Fregoli?" said Davy.

"Yes, I did. I do," Tom sniffed, wiping his nose on his sleeve. "I was hoping to catch up with him before he left."

"Now you can come to the ice harvest with us," said Billy.

Tom shrugged.

"You don't have to," said Davy. "You could stay and work with me. I could do with an assistant. I can't pay much, mind, but I'll feed you."

"You won't need to pay him," said Pop, with a note of jealousy in his voice. "He's got plenty of money. We've seen it."

"Why don't you stay, Tom? At least long enough to see how the film we shot today comes out. I've got a feeling the camera likes you – but you can never tell till you see it on screen." Davy realised that he might be offending the other two boys, and reluctantly risked making them the same offer. "You can help me too," he said, "If you can pay for your keep."

"No," said Pop, jumping in before Billy could speak. "We're going to the ice. That's proper work for a man."

"I'll miss you," said Tom, meaning it. He pulled out two five-dollar bills from his pocket, and gave Pop and Billy one each. "Here," he said. "That's for helping me along the way."

Davy smiled. "Save a bit to pay for a ticket to see him in the cinema one day."

"Sure," said Pop, dismissing the idea. "Now we'd better get on our way if we're going to find that North River."

"I can show you the road," said Davy, "Then Tom and I will get down to planning our next film."

So Tom said goodnight to Pop and Billy, and went to ask the barman for a room. Over supper, Davy bought Tom more beer than he had ever drunk at one sitting. As he staggered to bed, Tom had a vague sense that he had talked a lot, and possibly been rather repetitive about his angry disappointment with his father. He could recall little about Davy Payne, who must have done most of the listening.

18. NEWS FROM THE FACTORY

The manager at the silkworks was surprised by Harrison Bayfield's note instructing him to help Doctor Farcett set up a consulting room in the factory. Indeed, he was amazed to receive any communication from his boss at all. Bayfield had shown little interest in the business on inheriting it, and none at all since the fire. But orders were orders, and so a storeroom was cleared, and Farcett assembled a makeshift desk, screen and couch, ready to receive patients. He sat alone for a couple of hours before realising why no one had come. Though Mary had put up posters advertising his presence, the workers were frightened to leave their machines in case they got in trouble with their supervisors. So he pulled on his white coat, slung his stethoscope round his neck (removing the need to explain who he was) and set off into the dusty hubbub of the shop floor.

The workers, straining to make themselves heard over the noise of the machinery, spoke in a mixture of English and Italian. Many of them had brought their weaving skills from Europe in search of a better life. Others had come to do more menial work alongside their relatives. Farcett knew enough Italian to get the drift of what they were saying to each other, but he didn't want them to know that. He decided to speak only English himself, assuming (rightly, as it turned out) that the exchanges likely to be of most interest to Armitage would be conducted in the workers' mother tongue. He hoped they would feel free to talk among themselves in his presence.

Farcett introduced himself to the men and women while they worked: terrified and impressed by their dexterity as they laced strands of silk into the machines without getting their fingers sliced off. He marvelled at the strength of the men who humped huge bolts of finished cloth onto carts, and he patiently dealt with the disagreeable foreman as, one by one, the staff were allowed to leave their duties for a few minutes to consult him in the relative calm and privacy of his miniature surgery.

Medically, the story was interesting, but unsurprising – mainly the respiratory problems and skin rashes that Farcett had been led to expect. But as he gently nudged his patients to talk to him about conditions in the factory, the fire, and their hopes and fears for the future, he began to amass a little material that might be of interest to Armitage, and a great deal for his own study of a community under stress.

His last customer before the lunch break was Luisa Borro: an elderly woman – or rather a woman he assumed to be elderly until she gave him her date of birth, which revealed that she was barely forty. She was stooped and grey, thanks to her hard life in Paterson and before that in a similar sweat shop in her home town in Italy, where the sun had dried her skin into the wrinkled parchment he saw before him now. However, her medical problems couldn't be blamed entirely on her job. She had 'women's troubles' which might have afflicted a duchess of the same age. That was just a question of luck. Farcett gave her a bottle of iron tonic, which she was astounded, relieved and grateful to receive without charge. The klaxon sounded for the meal break.

Luisa smiled at Farcett. "Have you brought some food with you?"

Only then did Farcett realise that he should have, and that he was rather hungry.

"You can share mine, if you like," she said, taking a parcel wrapped in a handkerchief from her apron pocket.

She wouldn't take no for an answer, and Farcett followed her to a small courtyard in the middle of the factory, where the workers were gathering for their brief rest. As Luisa introduced him to her companions from the dyeing room, and (he thought) rather overplayed her testimony to his powers of healing, Farcett listened to the babble around him. A tight gathering of men in one corner was talking in animated Italian. As far as Farcett could make out, they were excited about the imminent arrival of a visitor to Paterson. His name seemed to be *Lo Zoppo*, and though Farcett couldn't quite catch the details of when he was expected, it was clear that for the Italians he was a legendary figure, and that they couldn't wait to see him in the flesh and to hear what he had to say. Farcett repeated the name in his head. *Lo Zoppo*, he thought. *Sounds like some sort of clown.* He couldn't blame the silk-workers for wanting entertainment after their hard labour at the factory – especially now that Fregoli was gone.

The afternoon's consultations reinforced Doctor Farcett's conviction that there was bubbling unrest at the factory. He had always prided himself on his ability to get his patients talking while he conducted physical examinations. Often it was this casual chat, helped along by the lack of eye contact as he tested reflexes and took measurements, that revealed what was really wrong with them. At the silkworks, persistent themes emerged: resentment at the pettiness of the foremen, who made no allowances for mistakes or calls of nature; the feeling that the workers were giving the best years of their lives for the enrichment of the Bayfield family without fair reward; a conviction – even a hope – that one day soon the bad feeling was bound to bubble up into something more. There was no indication that any action was planned, but one man (whom Farcett strongly suspected to be in the early stages of pneumonia) was more specific than most. After a discussion of working hours, Farcett had turned the conversation to the subject of the fire, hoping for material for his psychological study. A tone of even greater bitterness entered the man's voice.

"Of all the people to die that night," he said, shaking his head.

Farcett realised he was talking about Moretti, who had been masquerading as a librarian, but was in fact deeply involved in international anarchism, and in the death of Farcett's great friend Lord George Fox-Selwyn. Farcett placed his stethoscope on the man's back, though he had no need to listen any longer to his congested lungs.

"Yes. It was a blessing – even a miracle – that only one man died," said Farcett, disingenuously. "But to lose your librarian, and your library, must be a blow to you all."

The man grunted, setting off a bout of coughing, which echoed up though the stethoscope's earpieces. Farcett sensed that his patient was curbing himself from saying too much. For his own part, he felt he had successfully masked his special interest in Moretti, and any appreciation of what the implied reference to his importance might mean for political activists in Paterson.

Before leaving the factory at the end of the day, Farcett made extensive notes for himself about how his patients' mental equilibrium had been affected by recent events. He could already see how his article might shape up, and he was delighted that, with the material from the factory and his observations of Montmorency and Harrison Bayfield, all the social classes would be represented in his study. Then, aware that he had other obligations, he wrote a brief note to Armitage about the undercurrent of industrial discontent. He addressed it as they had arranged during their conversation at West Orange (a false name and an innocuous location) and, when he arrived back at the hotel, he gave it to the desk clerk to stamp and post.

Montmorency, returning from the soup kitchen, saw the doctor taking off his coat. "You look cheerful," he said. "How was your day at the factory?"

"Fascinating," said Farcett. He didn't want to talk to Montmorency about his psychological research, for fear that his friend would realise that he was under observation, so he confined himself to outlining the grievances of the workers. He was pretty confident that Armitage wouldn't mind the subject being discussed, as long as Farcett stuck by his promise not to reveal that he was investigating political unrest on behalf of the American secret service. Farcett talked about conditions in the factory, and described some of the skin and lung complaints they had caused. "Still," he added as an afterthought, "the people of Paterson have got something to look forward to. Apparently some sort of entertainer is on his way. *Lo Zoppo*, they call him. A clown, wouldn't you think, with a name like that?"

"Possibly," said Montmorency, though he had a feeling that *Zoppo* might have another meaning. "No doubt they could all do with cheering up."

"You too?" said Farcett, hoping, but not expecting, that his friend would say something to explain his persistent gloom.

"I'll just go and check on Tom," said Montmorency, setting off upstairs. He knew that Tom had an Italian dictionary somewhere in his room. The boy had wanted to learn the language in the hope of accompanying Fregoli back to his homeland. After a fruitless search of the tiny bookcase, Montmorency found the book tucked underneath the bed. He turned to the pages at the very back.

Zoppia: lameness.

Zoppicante: limping.

Zoppicare: to have a limp, to walk with a limp.

Zoppo: Limp. Lo Zoppo: the limping one… The cripple.

The one thing about Malpensa that could not be disguised.

Did Robert secretly know what the word meant? Was he, yet again, showing himself to be a much better undercover operator than Montmorency would have predicted? Was he passing on information to Montmorency under the noses of Armitage's agents, giving him a chance to get to Malpensa before they did? Montmorency sat on Tom's bed. He picked up a pullover from the floor, and sniffed it for a scent of the boy. Wherever Tom was, he could do with this jumper now, in the bitter winter cold.

Part of Montmorency rejoiced that with Malpensa about to arrive in Paterson, his son was out of the way; but what if he was lost, shivering in a freezing ditch, or lured into bad company? What if Malpensa heard that Tom was on the loose, and murdered him first, to inflict the worst of all tortures on Montmorency before killing him, too? News of Tom's flight must not leak out. Whatever happened, Montmorency had to sustain the conceit that the boy was still sulking in his room. He heard Frank talking to Robert downstairs, and pulled himself together, ready to go down to eat with them. For Tom's sake, he must keep the attention of Armitage's men firmly focussed on Malpensa's arrival in Paterson. As he entered the dining room, he instructed the waiter to leave Tom's meal on a tray outside his room.

"Tom still won't come down," he said to Robert and Frank, "I think it's best that we leave him up there until he feels ready to get off his high horse."

"I'll go up to him," said Frank. "He'll want to see this." Frank was holding a copy of the very newspaper Tom himself had read in Fort Lee. "He'll like the pictures of Fregoli. He's made the front page."

"No," snapped Montmorency, so fiercely that Frank lashed back.

"For God's sake! I'm only trying to help," he said, wounded by Montmorency's harshness.

"Can't you see that will only make things worse?"

"You're just pandering to him – letting him behave like a child to make up for ignoring him all these years!"

Montmorency was cut to the heart. He knew that Frank was right. He had failed to be a proper father to Tom, despite his good intentions. But he knew that the best he could do for his son now was to cover for him, so that no one – neither Armitage nor Malpensa – went in pursuit of him. He turned on his heels.

"You start eating without me. I'm going back up to make sure they've taken some food to him."

There was indeed a tray outside the door. Montmorency took it inside Tom's room, and – fighting tears – ate the chop, cabbage and potatoes. He wasn't hungry, but had to make sure that any of Armitage's informers amongst the kitchen staff believed that Tom was still there. And he knew that, when he was back downstairs, he must do all in his power to let Armitage's men know that Malpensa was definitely on his way to Paterson, without Frank guessing what his hints meant. The thought that what might be his last days with Frank were bathed in animosity and deceit only deepened Montmorency's gloom. If he was killed, Frank's freshest memories of him would be of a miserable liar, who had abandoned his son. But to explain what was going on would surely put Frank in danger from both Armitage and Malpensa. Montmorency longed for someone to share his torment with. He stroked the immobile mound in the centre of the bed. "What do you think, Tom, old chap?" he said, though a mouthful of apple pie and cream. "Am I doing the right thing? Do I have a choice?" There was no reply, of course. "At least I can do what I believe is the best for you, even if I may die before I have a chance to explain."

While Montmorency was upstairs, Farcett tried to calm Frank down, spelling out his concerns for Montmorency's mental health.

"You must go easy on him," said Robert. "Don't forget that he nearly died in that fight with Moretti."

"But that fight killed off the last of his enemies. Montmorency should be happy. He should be proud."

"Yes, but the fire has wrecked many lives. Perhaps he blames himself for starting it. Maybe he feels guilty."

"Well he shouldn't," said Frank. "If the people of Paterson knew who Moretti really was, they'd be grateful to Montmorency for making them safer than ever. In any case, they already admire him for what he and Mary are doing to help the hungry and the homeless. Where is Mary, anyway? She wasn't at the soup kitchen today."

"She's up at the Bayfield house," said Farcett, as Montmorency, who had placed the empty tray on the floor outside Tom's locked room, joined them at the table. Farcett continued, "Poor Harrison Bayfield's in a bad way. He's as much a victim of the fire as anyone else."

The waiter brought in Montmorency's plate, which had been kept warm in the kitchen because he was late for supper. The others watched as he picked at the edges, leaving more than half uneaten.

Frank, moved by Montmorency's evident distress, apologised. "I'm sorry, he said. I can see that you have had a hard day."

"No I haven't," said Montmorency, with a false jollity that frightened Frank and intrigued Doctor Farcett. "Others have life much worse." When the waiter returned with his pudding, he saw an opportunity to signal Malpensa's arrival to Armitage. "And after all," he said, much louder than necessary, "we have something to look forward to." He slapped the table, making the cutlery jangle. "*Lo Zoppo* is on his way!"

"Who's *Lo Zoppo*?" asked Frank.

Robert replied: "An Italian clown, I think." But he was really wondering why Montmorency seemed more interested in the arrival of a circus entertainer than in Mary's failure to show her face at the hotel that night.

19. $\mathcal{I}$N THE MOVIES

Tom slept badly, wondering whether he should stay with the film-maker, go to the ice field with Pop and Billy, or take a chance and hope that he had enough money left for a ticket on a ship to Europe. In the early hours he decided on the ice harvest, and he meant to get up at dawn to beg his new friends to take him with them after all but, just before sunrise, he fell into the deepest of sleeps.

When he awoke there was no sign of Pop and Billy – not even a note saying goodbye. He was surprised how hurt he was. Even after such a short (and at times stressful) acquaintance he found himself concerned for their safety, and wishing them well. Clearly they hadn't felt the same. Worrying about the boys stirred his conscience. How much more anxious must Montmorency and the others be back in Paterson? Tom was still angry with them all, and especially with Montmorency, but even he could imagine the possibilities of death and disaster that must be flashing though their minds since his disappearance. He decided to write a letter to Frank – not giving away where he was, or apologising, but at least showing that he was still alive. He went down to the hotel reception desk to ask for a pen and paper, but before he had the chance to start writing, Davy Payne appeared with a letter of his own, and a look of great excitement.

"Oh happy, happy chance!" he exclaimed, waving the envelope. His mood could not have been at greater variance from Tom's.

"It's all right for you," Tom said. "Billy and Pop have gone off without me. They've left without even saying goodbye."

Davy Payne sat on the edge of Tom's table. "You don't want to waste your time worrying about those two," he said. "I could tell they were no good."

"They were my friends," said Tom. "They helped me when I was all alone."

"And you helped them. I saw you give them money last night."

"It was the least I could do," said Tom. "And I should be with them now – off to do honest work on the ice harvest."

"I thought you were set on following your friend Fregoli."

"Once I've got enough money, yes. They say the pay's good at the ice field."

"In return for hard labour," said Payne. "And then you have to hold on to it. There's nothing to do up there except drink and play cards. The bottle and the poker take a man's wages faster than any woman. You could work there for months with nothing to show for it but an aching back and an empty wallet."

"But like Pop said, it's proper men's work. And I would have saved the money."

"If you say so. But what if I told you there was another way to get to travel – and at someone else's expense?"

"I'd say you were trying to trick me into something."

"I'm not, honestly. And if you ask me, those boys have done you a favour by slinking off without you. Forget them, and stay with me."

"To do what? Prance around in front of your camera? You told me yesterday that you couldn't pay me much. What's all this about travel all of a sudden?"

Davy dropped the letter onto the table. "Read that," he said. "It's from an old friend of mine in Canada, Jim Freebody. You must have heard of him. You come from London, don't you?"

"No. And no. I've lived in London, but I don't come from there. I was born on an island off the west coast of Scotland…"

"OK, OK. But you're a Brit, aren't you? Jim Freebody had a big hit there in '99. He toured showing his films."

"I was just a child then."

Davy Payne smiled. Tom seemed little more than a child to him now, but he realised that when you're in your early teens a couple of years seems like an age, and that your younger self is something to be looked back on with smug contempt. "Well, take it from me, Jim Freebody was quite a sensation. The Canadian Pacific Railway paid him to make films about life in Canada so that people would want to visit and ride their trains. It worked, and now they've asked him to do it again."

"What's that got to do with me – or you, for that matter?"

"He's asked me to help him. I was his assistant on some of his early films. He taught me all I know – well, all the technical stuff, at least. I like to think I'm a bit more artistic than him."

"I still don't see where I come in."

"I'm getting to that." Payne took the letter out of the envelope and read a bit to Tom. Freebody, who was based in Manitoba, didn't want to take the same old films to Europe a second time. They had been mostly of the countryside around his home. He wanted more from the east of Canada – the part that tourists from Europe would encounter first. But Freebody's wife was heavily pregnant ("Yet again," laughed Payne) and he didn't want to leave her, so he was suggesting that Payne should provide him with material to fill the gap.

"So here's the deal," said Payne, reading more slowly. "*Canadian Pacific will provide free travel on their trains for you and an assistant. Make sure you get plenty of shots of trains, as well of the landscape around you. You know the stuff I like!"*

Tom was silent.

Payne thought he didn't understand. "Me, and an assistant. I'm asking you if you want to come. We can travel across Canada for free. And while we're filming Freebody's landscapes for him, we can do some work of our own – those dramas we were talking about last night. We can sell them on to picture houses. Canada will give us all the backdrops we need, I can tell you. And if you're looking for ice fields, I can guarantee them. You just won't have to dig them up. What do you say?"

"But we'll be going from east to west. It's the wrong direction. How will I catch up with Fregoli?"

"Listen, Tom. I didn't want to say this when we were talking last night – with you so upset, and all…" (Tom realised that he might have revealed more than he thought in that drink-fuelled conversation) "…but think about it. Is it really such a good idea to chase Fregoli half way round the world? Did he wait for you? Will he even remember you, or take any notice of you when he's back amongst his own people?"

Tom tried to interrupt to say *yes, of course*, but in truth, a little doubt was dawning in his mind. Payne ploughed on, playing on Tom's image of himself as an independent adult. Fregoli himself had laid the groundwork for that to be a particularly successful approach.

"Isn't it time for you to go your own way?" said Payne. "Isn't that why you left your folks back in Paterson? I told you. The camera loves you. Believe me, that's a magic no one can teach. I can put you in front of it – in exchange for you helping out behind it, too. And if we play our cards right, who knows, Canadian Pacific might pay for us to go to Europe with Freebody. I'm not promising anything, but it could happen. Then you could track down Fregoli, and prove me wrong." He flashed a smile. "What do you say?"

Tom took a beat too long to reply.

Payne folded his letter and tucked the envelope back in his pocket. "Oh, well," he sighed, "If back-breaking work in the ice fields of the North River appeals more. Or maybe you were thinking of going back to Paterson with your tail between your legs?"

Tom took the bait. "No, no," he stammered, fearing that Payne was withdrawing his offer. "No. I'd love to come. It's just a bit of a shock…"

"Well, get over it, because we're leaving for Quebec this afternoon. Shall we shake on it?" He held out his hand. "Welcome aboard, Tom…" Payne faltered. "I nearly called you Tom Payne," he laughed, "but you must have a name of your own?"

"Evans," said Tom. "Tom Evans." After the way Montmorency had treated him in Paterson he was determined to revert to his old surname.

"Right then, Tom Evans. Your first job is to help me pack the gear. It's valuable stuff, and there's no way we can replace things or get them mended when we're on the road. I'm going to teach you how to take good care of every piece of kit. Play your cards right, and I'll show you how to use it, too. By the time all this is over, I will have turned you into the best assistant cameraman in the business."

Tom looked down at the blank sheet of paper in front of him. He hadn't even begun his letter to Frank. He picked up his pen, but Payne interrupted him.

"That can wait till later, whatever it is. We've got to get moving."

"Yes, sir," said Tom.

"And when we've got the equipment in order, we'll go out and buy you some warm clothes," said Payne. "It'll be pretty chilly where we're going, I can tell you."

"I've heard of Quebec," said Tom. "We did it in History at school. It's where General Wolfe smashed the French in 1759."

"That's not the way a lot of the Quebecois see it!" said Payne. "You'd better watch what you say about all your English generals. Even round here they're not so keen on them. Best just to keep your mouth shut about where you come from, and enjoy the trip."

Once he got used to the idea, Tom couldn't wait to reach the promised land of high mountains, wide rivers and rushing trains that lay ahead of him. When he had finished cleaning and packing Payne's equipment, he dashed off his letter to Frank, less concerned now with calming any worries than with making Frank jealous of the new excitement in his life. He imagined that with Fregoli gone, life in Paterson would have settled into a calm equilibrium of polite meals and good works. In fact, the scene was rather different.

20. SECRET GIFTS

In the days that followed his first visit to the factory, Doctor Farcett, fired up with enthusiasm for his covert political and overt medical tasks, was the happiest of the Paterson party. Frank, busy at the soup kitchen by day, and playing cards with the hotel staff by night, grew increasingly impatient with Tom's insistence on staying in his room, and with Montmorency's stubbornness and lack of appetite (though he blamed them both on Tom). Every newspaper brought a more exaggerated account of the philanthropic work the British visitors were doing in Paterson, always including Montmorency's picture. Montmorency himself expected Malpensa, lured by the press coverage, to appear at any moment, and his unexplained edginess got on everyone's nerves. Eventually, alone with Farcett in the breakfast room, he cracked. That morning's paper had yet another colour piece on the soup kitchen, with a photo of Montmorency and Mary, ladles in hand.

"Why Mary?" Montmorency shouted, throwing the paper across the table. "Why does she have to be in the picture?"

He instantly regretted his outburst, for two reasons. Firstly, it was unfair to force Farcett to talk about Armitage's use of the press when he was doing such a good job disguising his knowledge of what was going on. Secondly, Mary arrived in the room just as the newspaper landed in the butter.

Montmorency knew she must have heard his words, and that the only way she could interpret them was as the jealousy of a proud self-publicist, reluctant to share the limelight. How could he explain that he was really concerned for her safety? Neither he nor the doctor filled the embarrassed silence. It was left to Mary to behave as if nothing had happened.

"I just dropped by to explain that I may be a little late at the soup kitchen this morning," she said. "I have some business elsewhere in town."

Montmorency, still stunned, said nothing. Farcett forced a smile. "Not to worry. I'm going there this morning, so I can lend a hand with preparing the food if you are delayed." He overdid an attempt to make it sound like a good idea. "I'd like to see what goes into the soup, anyway," he said, unconvincingly. "You know how interested I am in nutrition."

"Thank you. Must be off," said Mary, her voice pitched unusually high.

She had left the building before Montmorency composed himself. Without saying a word to Farcett, he went upstairs, unlocked Tom's room, and slumped down on the bed, cursing Malpensa for taking so long to come.

Mary, who actually had no plans other than to go to the soup kitchen as normal, made her way instead up the hill to Harrison Bayfield's house. She felt guilty that she hadn't been back since her visit with Doctor Farcett, despite their agreement that Bayfield should not be left alone for too long. It was early enough for him to be sober, and he welcomed her with grace, though still overcome with gloom.

"I have a little time on my hands," said Mary. "I wondered if there was anything I could do to help you here."

"How kind," said Bayfield. "But please, Miss Gibson, I find it hard to believe that you are at a loose end. I know how busy you have been, seeing to the needs of those affected by the fire.

In fact, I envy you your sense of purpose. Your life is worth living. Mine is truly pointless."

"Oh, I'm sure not," said Mary. "You and your enterprises are important to a great many people."

"Important? Well, if so, not in a good way. Come in and take a look."

Harrison Bayfield took Mary to his study, where the desk was piled high with unopened letters. "I have no secretary now. He left some weeks ago. As I may have let slip the other day, I wouldn't be able to pay him had he stayed. But the truth is it was me, and not the lack of money, that drove him away."

Mary ignored the implied invitation to come out with a polite contradiction of Bayfield's self-criticism. She sensed that the only way to lift his mood was to attend to practicalities.

"So you don't know what's inside all these envelopes?" she asked.

"It doesn't take a genius to guess. Bills. Complaints from angry customers of the insurance business. Ultimatums from people I once thought were my friends."

"But there may be other things too. Maybe some good news. And even if you are right, nothing will get better if you just pretend that your problems don't exist. Tell me, would it be too much of an intrusion if I were to sort out this paperwork for you?"

"I couldn't possibly..."

"Please. I wouldn't offer if I didn't mean it. Why don't you go and freshen up for the day while I get started, and then perhaps we can talk through whatever I find?"

Bayfield was touched by the tact with which she had noted his dishevelled state, and calmly took himself off for a bath and a shave while Mary picked up a silver letter-opener, and set to work. Much of the correspondence was as predicted by Bayfield, but there was something else amidst the invoices and threats of legal action: an invitation from the Mayor of Paterson for Bayfield to take part in a ceremony to open the first public building restored after the fire. There was to be a parade through the town on Sunday week, starting from the station and making its way to the church, where craftsmen and parishioners had worked tirelessly to fix the roof, replace the charred pews, and redecorate the altar ready to resume worship.

"It seems that they want you to help plan the event," said Mary, as Bayfield returned, shaven and dressed to face the day.

Bayfield dismissed the idea that the Mayor valued his organisational skills. "I know how to read between the lines. What they're really after is money. Where am I going to find that?" He shook his head. "I've got nothing to give."

Mary's voice, though still kindly, took on a sterner note. "Yes you have! You can give your time. And look at the date," she tried to pass the letter to him, but he turned away. "It was written yesterday. It seems that the city fathers have only just decided to hold the parade at all. And who can blame them for being a bit disorganised? They really have been working hard since the fire. I think they genuinely need someone to take the lead and make the commemoration happen."

Bayfield's reedy despair was replaced by a more forceful insistence that he was in no condition to help Paterson overcome its difficulties: "Don't you understand? I can't face seeing those people. I don't know what's worse, their joy at my unhappiness, or their pity. I won't be joining in their day of civic pride."

"You make it sound as if its only purpose is to humiliate you. Don't you think the townspeople deserve a bit of colour in their lives?"

"Not at my expense. Just put the letter on the fire."

"But you must reply. Are you sure that you can't give them even a little money in recompense for being unable to join them?"

"I've told you. I have absolutely nothing to offer the people of Paterson!" Mary could barely stifle a laugh, and Bayfield looked up at her in surprise. "You don't believe me?" he asked.

"Oh, I believe that you can't put your hands on cash right away," said Mary, "But look around you. This house must be full of things that victims of the fire would find useful: bedding, clothes, pieces of furniture that have outlived their usefulness..."

"I don't need any of it. It's all just part of my burden now."

"Then shed that load," said Mary. "Give your possessions to people who really have lost everything, and are struggling through the winter without proper shelter or clothes. I could take things to the soup kitchen or the factory, and give them away there."

"And have my workforce think I'm trying to buy them off with charity?"

"No one need know where the gifts have come from. You would simply be doing some good." Harrison looked thoughtful at the unfamiliar concept of anonymous philanthropy. Mary continued, "I can assure you, it will make you feel better. And what if you don't do it? To be honest with you, it seems from some of these letters that your creditors may be coming sooner than you think to take away the contents of this house. Would you rather your possessions went to the bank, or to people who can barely sleep through the night because they're so cold?"

Bayfield struggled to find an argument against what Mary proposed. He was so used to self-disgust that could hardly imagine feeling privately proud of himself. "I still don't want to get tangled up in that parade," he said.

"Are you sure?" said Mary. "If the Mayor wants you to be involved in the re-opening of the church, maybe it's to set an example. He probably thinks your name will attract others to take part: to give money to help restore other buildings and pull Paterson back up again." She smiled. "However low your opinion of yourself might be right now, I'm afraid you just have to accept that other people think you have your uses." Bayfield grunted contemptuously, but Mary took no notice. "Helping to commemorate Paterson's recovery from the fire might be just what you need."

"I can't. I simply can't." Bayfield seized a handful of invoices and waved them in the air. "I've got no money to give, and I won't be able to show my face if I haven't contributed to the cost of the parade. In any case, I simply don't want to go. Why should I stand around in the cold while that windbag of a mayor makes one of his speeches? I'll end up sick, as well as bankrupt."

Mary fell quiet for a moment, then spoke slowly. "Maybe you've hit on a solution," she said. "Yes, I have an idea." She was thinking about Robert's concerns for Bayfield, and as she spoke a plan seemed to fall into place. "You could send the Mayor a letter, saying that you are unwell, but that you are anxious to help." Bayfield tried to demur, but Mary held up her hand to stop him. "Please. Hear me out. I could ask Doctor Farcett to come to see you a couple of times a day for the rest of the week. I know he enjoys your company, and that in any case he would like to talk to you about the health of your workforce. Word that he was visiting would be bound to spread around town. People would believe that you could not take part in the parade."

"But they would still want money."

"I'm coming to that. The letter could also say that you regret not being fit to lend a hand yourself, but that you will endow a committee of ladies to organise the parade, and that you have asked me to take the lead."

Bayfield interrupted, "But I can't..."

"Don't worry about the money. My mother left me plenty. No one need know that the funds don't come from you."

"But I couldn't possibly ask you to lend me money."

"It wouldn't be a loan to you." said Mary. "It would be a gift from me to Paterson – and in return, you would be giving me a means of contributing anonymously. Believe me, I have no need of any more attention than I already get, thanks to the newspapers. I would be happier to do it this way, and happier still to think that you would keep the respect of people in this town."

"And this committee of ladies…?"

Mary was reassuring. "Leave it to me. I know who to call upon."

"You have the time to do all this?"

"I can make the time. It's only for a few days, and I will welcome the change from doling out soup. That operation is up and running nicely now. I'm sure my maid can take my place there." Mary didn't mention (in fact, she didn't really admit to herself) that she would be glad to have a good reason to spend less time with her English friends for a while. She clapped her hands and smiled. "What do you say? Shall we get that letter written right now?"

Bayfield sighed, but Mary was firm. She knew that if she backed down, Harrison would simply sag back into his despair, and in any case, she was already composing a mental list of congenial women who might help give Paterson a day to remember. She found a pen underneath the detritus on the desk, and a bottle of ink in one of the drawers. After a few false starts, the two of them were absorbed in composing the note – laughing together about how to strike exactly the right tone to tickle the Mayor's vanity while ensuring that he would feel flattered by Bayfield's attention, and keen to accept his proposal.

When the envelope had been sealed, Harrison helped Mary select the first of the donated clothes from wardrobes in his guest bedrooms. He had never disposed of garments left behind by his late brother's widow, Cissie. There was plenty to choose from, and it was good quality, if a little out of style. Mary borrowed a wheelbarrow from the gardener's hut, and took the first batch down to the soup kitchen in time for the lunchtime rush. Her spirits were high now, and higher still when Doctor Farcett received with undisguised delight the suggestion that he should make several visits to Harrison. He had been trying to think up ways of engineering encounters so that he could find out more about Bayfield's psychological plight. Now he was being positively encouraged to call at the big house whenever he could. It was too good an opportunity to miss.

Montmorency was pleased to see that Mary was cheerful. He persuaded himself that she might not have heard his apparent harsh words that morning. He set to work helping her set up a table to display the clothes while she explained about her plans for the women's committee and next Sunday's big parade. Word had gone round the soup queue that warm woollens might be on offer, and a small crowd was gathering at the mouth of the tent, ready to swoop.

As Mary chattered on about bunting, baking and brass bands, Montmorency found himself eavesdropping on a conversation in Italian between two young men at one edge of the chaotic queue. It was the word *Zoppo* that caught his attention. Then *Domenica* – Sunday – less than a week away. So, Malpensa was on his way. There was a strange relief in knowing that the wait would not go on much longer.

Montmorency listened harder, and shuffled closer to the men, hoping to catch more details. Mary looked up from folding the clothes, and saw only his disengagement from her. By the time he returned his attention to the charity table, Mary's head was down again and, though he could not tell as she laid out the scarves, socks and pullovers, her heart was back in her boots.

Montmorency felt more certain than ever that she, with her quiet dignity and selfless concern for the community, was the woman with whom he should share his life. Should he ask her now to set a date for their marriage? He wanted nothing more than for the two of them to become one. But he knew that, if he had understood the fragments of conversation correctly, he might be offering no more than an invitation to instant widowhood. So he held his tongue, and let the cold and hungry horde into the tent.

21. *Escape?*

Two days later, there was more post. Montmorency, having accomplished his new routine of eating Tom's breakfast and rear-ranging the sleeping dummy, went downstairs to the sound of laughter from the dining room. It was too late for Montmorency to check the envelope to see whether the letter Frank was reading to Robert had been intercepted by Armitage's men. In any case, Frank's voice was so loud that any of the waiters would be able to pass on every detail.

Frank stopped as Montmorency entered the room. "It's from Alexander," he said. "It seems that Angelina's pregnancy is progressing well now, and he's had news from Dad at home. Tell you what – I might as well go back to the beginning."

For a moment, Montmorency feared that his subterfuge was about to be exposed. Alex and Frank's father, Gus, Duke of Monaburn, might well have passed on the news that Malpensa was still alive and believed to be at large in the United States. It would be entirely natural for him to write about the true identity of the man they had mistaken for Malpensa. Montmorency braced himself for Frank reading out news of the charming American agent now staying as a welcome house guest at Glendarvie Castle in Scotland. He knew that Frank would fly into a wild rage if the letter revealed how far – and how deliberately – he had been misled.

But it soon became clear that Alexander was obeying Armitage's instructions. He had not enclosed Gus's letter, but had paraphrased it, carefully restricting the news to family gossip. So the meat of the letter was about how the Duke and Beatrice, his Duchess, planned a spring trip to Italy, and how thrilled they would be if Frank, Montmorency, Farcett and Tom would join them all at Beatrice's palazzo in Florence. Tom's mother, Vi Evans, would be there too.

Frank did not even try to disguise his joy at the prospect of leaving Paterson. "Tom will love to see his mother again," he said. "If this doesn't cheer him up, nothing will. Who knows, we might even run into Fregoli. I'll take this up to him right away."

Montmorency, who by now was helping himself to tiny portions of food at the sideboard, could do nothing to stop Frank bounding from the room. "Just slide it under his door," he shouted. "He's locked himself in again." He discreetly checked his pocket, to make sure he hadn't left the key behind.

The noise of Frank banging on Tom's door and berating him for his childish sulk rang round the hotel for a good five minutes.

Doctor Farcett was concerned. "Maybe I should have a look at Tom," he said.

"No need," said Montmorency, "he's not ill. He's just got everything a bit out of proportion."

"Perhaps the letter will help," said Farcett.

"Very likely," said Montmorency, shouting again to Frank, "Just give up. I've promised that we won't force him to open the door. Slip the letter underneath. It might do some good."

And indeed, thought Montmorency, in normal circumstances it could have worked. Tom would have been excited by the idea of travelling to Fregoli's home nation. For the rest of them, the delights of revisiting one of Europe's most beautiful cities at the most pleasant season of the year would inevitably be shaded with sadness. It was in Florence that they had met Lord George Fox-Selwyn's killer, Moretti, and become embroiled in the maelstrom of international anarchism that still threatened them all. But even so, the trip would be preferable to being trapped here in America, waiting, powerless, for Malpensa to arrive.

Montmorency played with the idea of grasping this way out of Paterson. Maybe, if he could find Tom, they would all go, just as Gus suggested, and he could restart his relationship with his growing son amidst the delights of Tuscany. They would muffle the anguish of the past with gracious architecture, soft light, smooth wine, music, art, and hope. Montmorency cursed himself for letting Armitage dictate his actions. Even though he knew he had no real choice if the others were to be safe, he felt weak and humiliated. He thought back to earlier times – dashing across Europe with George Fox-Selwyn, ignoring authorities of any nationality, defying terrorists from Ireland and Italy, and facing down Malpensa himself with no help from anyone else. Even before all that, he had risked his life in London, playing the parts of a toff and his servant, and managing to keep them both safe, despite one of the biggest police hunts of the day. Now here he was, living pampered in an American hotel – needing all his bravery, but forbidden to use any of his initiative, and with no hope of recognition for a mission that might cost him his life. Why didn't he just leave and look for Tom? Isn't that what any other father would do? Did he have the right to consider himself to be a parent at all if he didn't put Tom first? And weren't his skills especially suited to the search? Surely he could concoct a disguise that would fool even the American secret service. He could leave town without them knowing.

Montmorency looked at his reflection in the silver dome that covered a dish of pancakes on the sideboard. A tired, ageing man stared back. He had little doubt that with a few theatrical make-up tricks, and some alterations to the way he held his body, walked and talked, he would be able to pass as someone much older – perhaps an immigrant from a foreign land who couldn't speak English at all. He envied Frank the instant transformation he had once made simply by changing his hair colour from red to black. Light to dark was easy. For Montmorency it would be more of a challenge: he might be greying slightly at the temples, but most of his head was covered with the lustrous dark-brown thatch which had inspired admiration in women and jealousy in men throughout his adult life. To change his hair he would need bleach. Or perhaps he could just shave his head completely, to complete the elderly look.

"Aren't you ever going to come to the table?" asked Farcett, breaking Montmorency's reverie. "You've been over there for ages, and you still have hardly anything on your plate."

"Sometimes you can have too much choice," said Montmorency, spooning a few mushrooms alongside his grilled tomatoes. He sat down and reluctantly picked up his knife and fork.

"I'm getting worried about your appetite," said Farcett. "That's hardly what I'd call a breakfast. I've known love-struck girls drop in weight, but a grown man like you should be able to cope with affairs of the heart!"

"I'm just not that hungry," said Montmorency, resenting the flippant reference to Mary, but once again admiring Farcett's ability to restrain himself from talking about their wider predicament even when he and Montmorency were alone. He took Farcett's lead, and stayed with the subject of food. "And I'm not losing weight, by the way. If the buckle on my belt is anything to go by, I'm getting bigger."

It was true. Gobbling down Tom's food every day, and then facing his own portion, was beginning to have the inevitable effect. But even Montmorency had to admit that his face was looking more drawn. He couldn't remember when he had last felt truly happy, or enjoyed a night's sleep free from care. It wasn't so much the presence of danger that was wearing him down – he had lived with that for years – it was the lack of hope. He needed to feel that he wasn't trapped into obeying Armitage: that he had a genuine option of defiance.

When Doctor Farcett finished his breakfast and left the room, Montmorency slipped out of the hotel and walked to the drug store. There he bought a bottle of hydrogen peroxide – a powerful antiseptic, but also an effective lightener for hair. He clasped it in his hand all the way home: a precious symbol of the possibility of escape. He just had time to return to his room and hide it in the chamber pot under his bed before dashing off to the soup kitchen. Montmorency's work there was becoming almost routine: the closest thing to a regular job he had ever experienced. He felt an itch to break away and do something less humdrum, and yet he knew he ought to treasure the luxury of the ordinary day that lay ahead. After all, it might well be one of his last.

As it turned out, the events of that day weren't at all predictable. Just as the soup was coming to a healthy simmer, someone ran into the tent frantically calling for Doctor Farcett. Seconds later, two more arrived, cradling a bloodied body between them. The man, swooning with shock, had caught his arm in the relentless machinery of an unguarded loom at the silkworks. Montmorency helped hold the victim down as Farcett did all he could to save the man's limb – and his life – much as he must have done all those years ago, when Montmorency had suffered the accident that changed his world.

It was a long and messy battle. Despite the doctor's insistence that he and his patient needed space and air, a crowd gathered round them, unable to take their eyes off the grisly scene.

They cursed in Italian about conditions in the factory, and how something must be done, soon, to punish Bayfield and improve the lives of the workers. Montmorency clearly heard the words *Zoppo* and *Domenica* again.

At first there was hope, as Farcett closed and cleaned the wound, but the blood loss was too great. When the man slumped into death, a chant built up, and though Montmorency couldn't understand precisely what it meant, he sensed that the mob might set off up the hill to lynch Harrison Bayfield. Farcett feared they would seize the body, and carry it with them. In English, he tried to calm the angry men, but they took no notice until Luisa Borro, the woman who had been so impressed by Farcett's medical skill, shouted at them in ferocious Italian, like a mother chiding naughty boys. She sent one of the ringleaders for a priest.

Chastened, the men gave Farcett and Luisa room to work, as they gently rearranged the corpse in a dignified pose, and covered it with a fine linen sheet from Mary's latest heap of donations from the big house.

Frank had called the police and, arriving late enough to miss the worst of the agitation, they marshalled the crowd to eat their soup outside the tent. Montmorency, drained, sat on a sack of potatoes, but Doctor Farcett calmly cleared away the bloody debris of his efforts, drew up a chair and spent several minutes making an extensive entry in his notebook. At first, Montmorency assumed that Robert was noting the medical details of the incident – perhaps to protect himself from any allegations that his actions had caused, or advanced, the man's death; but looking across, and reading upside-down, it seemed to Montmorency that the note included several references to the anger of the crowd, and their threats to Harrison Bayfield.

"You heard what they said about *Lo Zoppo* coming on Sunday?" said Montmorency, when he was sure that everyone else had left the tent.

"Yes," said Farcett, without raising his head. "Could be next Sunday, I think. Isn't that what 'dopo' means? Or perhaps *Doppo* is another comedian: *Doppo* and *Zoppo*. It has a certain ring to it. Still, it's odd that they should still be talking about clowns at a time like this. Very interesting indeed."

Montmorency was thrown by his friend's reply. Had he really not made the connection between *Lo Zoppo* and Malpensa? Was he talking in code, for fear of them being overheard? Or was he so obsessed with his medical study that he was deaf to the political significance of what had been said?

Later, back at the hotel, Montmorency saw Farcett give the desk clerk a letter to post. He thought nothing of it at the time. He was more concerned about the doctor's reaction to losing a patient so publicly.

"Can I help in any way?" he asked his friend, "You look done in."

"Well," said Farcett, "I do have to re-stock my medical bag. If I were to write a list, could you possibly go to the drug store and buy me what I need?"

"Of course," said Montmorency, grateful that he could be of use – and pleased that his earlier purchase of hydrogen peroxide might seem less suspicious, now that he was obviously shopping on behalf of the doctor.

When Montmorency returned, Farcett was asleep in a chair by the fire. His bag was at his side. Montmorency opened it quietly, to slip the bandages and painkiller inside. He spotted the notebook, and thought it would do no harm to read Robert's account of what had happened. After all, he had been there throughout, so the information could hardly be considered confidential. He knew that Robert had not confined himself to medical detail. What if he had said too much about the political unrest? What if this was some sort of diary where he unburdened himself about the threats from Armitage and Malpensa? Maybe that was why Robert was able to maintain such a calm exterior in the face of danger. But what if the book fell into the wrong hands? Montmorency had to know what was in it. He flicked through, unable to make much sense of the jargon and figures cramped onto the pages in Farcett's tiny handwriting. Then, after a heading showing that day's date, and a couple of routine entries about early patients, there was nothing except the jagged edges of six pages. The sheets recording the death had been removed. Had one of Armitage's men taken them? Had Farcett himself torn them out and put them on the fire? Why?

Montmorency was about to wake his friend, to tell him that his bag might have been tampered with, when he remembered Farcett's letter. Had Robert sent the report to someone? Was he trying to warn Harrison Bayfield of the threats against him? But why by post? Robert saw Bayfield every day now. He would be alone with him again before a letter could be delivered. Was there someone else who might be interested? Armitage perhaps? But Armitage had spies everywhere. He would know the latest news already. What about Malpensa? Surely he was the only person who would benefit from knowing for certain that Montmorency was aware of his imminent arrival. That would explain why Farcett pretended to think that *Lo Zoppo* was a clown. It all fitted. Montmorency didn't want to believe it, but it could be true. His friend might be set on betraying him.

But why would he do such a thing? Surely the only reason could be that Malpensa had some sort of hold over Robert. Blackmail? Or was Malpensa controlling him by the same method Armitage was using on Montmorency – with threats to hurt someone else unless he co-operated? But who might that be? The doctor had no loved ones as far as Montmorency knew. Then he thought of Tom – somewhere out there, alone and vulnerable. Maybe Malpensa had found him and was using him to get close to Montmorency – perhaps within killing distance of Harrison Bayfield, too. Farcett loved Tom like a son, and Montmorency knew that. If it was a choice between Montmorency, with all his faults, and Tom, who had a life ahead of him, which would Robert choose? Montmorency, looking into his own soul, had no doubt that he was less deserving than his son. He should be sacrificed for Tom's sake.

Leaving the doctor asleep in the chair, Montmorency went to the front desk. The clerk told him that the mail had been collected. He could not remember – or said he could not remember – to whom Doctor Farcett's letter had been addressed.

Montmorency tried to sound unconcerned. "Not to worry," he said. "It couldn't matter less."

The gong went for supper. Bemused, and too tired to think straight, Montmorency climbed the stairs to Tom's room. As he picked his way through the boy's meal, he cursed himself for being suspicious of Farcett – the man who had saved his life, and stood by him through good times and bad. He cursed Armitage too, for making him so nervous that it was possible for him to doubt his closest friend. Enough bad things were happening without inventing new ones. With relief, Montmorency realised that the best plan of action was the most honest and straightforward. He should simply own up to having looked at the notebook, and ask Farcett whether he knew that his report on the incident was gone, and if so, why.

He placed the empty tray outside Tom's door, and went downstairs as usual to eat his second supper. Frank was already at the table.

"Where's Robert?" asked Montmorency.

Sullenly scooping soup into his mouth, Frank hardly looked up. "Too tired to eat. He's gone to bed."

"I'm not surprised," said Montmorency. He could see that Frank was spoiling for another argument about Tom, and he couldn't face it, so he took the opportunity to get away. He pretended to yawn, but his fake yawn turned into a real one. "What a day," he said. "I think I'll turn in too."

Resolving to talk to Farcett in the morning, Montmorency fell asleep almost at once. In the early hours, he felt a call of nature and reached under the bed for his chamber pot. There was a piece of paper inside, with a scrawled message in capital letters: *DON'T EVEN THINK OF DOING IT.* Don't even think of doing what? Then, more fully awake, Montmorency remembered the hydrogen peroxide. The bottle was gone. Someone knew he was contemplating an escape from Paterson in disguise. One of Armitage's spies on the hotel staff? He looked for a clue in the handwriting. It could be anyone's. His suspicion and confusion returned and multiplied. Could it be Farcett – primed by Armitage or Malpensa to keep Montmorency in the line of fire? How could he be sure that Frank was not in on the plot, or even Mary? How could he tell? Was there any way of finding out? How could he trust anyone? Lying in bed on that cold winter night, Montmorency could be sure of only two things. He felt more alone than ever, and Malpensa – *Lo Zoppo* – was on his way.

22. MONTMORENCY FALLS

While Farcett was struggling to save the factory worker in Paterson, Tom was far to the north, in Canada, gazing at a mighty waterfall, frozen solid by the winter chill. Happy families were tobogganing down its lower slopes, skaters were weaving across the lake at the bottom, and Davy Payne was setting up his camera to film the fun. Tom couldn't help but be impressed by the beauty around him: the falls, though narrower than Niagara, were higher, and made the thundering power source at Paterson look tiny. But it wasn't the sight of this natural wonder that set Tom's brain spinning. It was its name. For these were the Montmorency Falls, dropping down from the Montmorency River, and however absorbed he was in stabilising the tripod and cleaning the lens, his mind was on the surname he had rejected, his father and his friends.

Payne asked a small boy if he could borrow his sledge in return for a look down the viewfinder.

"Here you are, Tom," he said, handing the toboggan over. "I'll get a few shots of you sliding down. Go as high as you can and set off when you see me wave my arm."

Tom carried the sledge up the slippery bank, still distracted by thoughts of Montmorency, Frank and Farcett back in Paterson. His letter couldn't have got there yet. They must be wondering where he was. Were they looking for him? Even if they were, where would they search? Not here, surely. Maybe Montmorency had contacted Fregoli before he's embarked, to see whether Tom had caught up with him. Tom wondered whether Fregoli, out on the ocean, was worried too, or if he had put Tom out of his mind, just as Payne had said he would? Maybe he had found another keen young boy to help him with his props and costumes. Perhaps no one could be bothered to search for Tom. Maybe his friends had taken the obvious message from his rage back in Paterson, and accepted that he wanted to break away from them all and live his own life. That was just how he had wanted them to react when he'd flounced out of their lives, but he found the thought of such indifference strangely disappointing now.

Tom placed the sledge on the ice and stepped from the bank to climb aboard, but he wasn't concentrating, and his feet slid beneath him. For a couple of seconds he slithered awkwardly, trying to lower his bottom onto the seat. At the last moment, a gust of wind caught his hat, and he raised his hand to catch it, just in time. But his hand had been holding the sledge, and it took off without him, leaving him sitting on the ice. He reached forward in a pathetic attempt to stop the sledge, succeeding only in propelling himself forward, head over heels, gathering momentum all the time. By pure chance he avoided crashing into other toboggans, swishing past his ears. Then, spread-eagled, he gradually spun to stop on the frozen lake at the bottom of the slope, losing his hat again. A skater swerved into a sharp turn to avoid him, throwing up a shower of icy shards, almost like a firework.

Once he had his breath back, Tom struggled to get up, like a newborn calf trying to find its legs for the first time. Steady at last, he saw his hat lying on the ice, and made a graceful swoop to pick it up. He slapped it back on his head, only to find himself suddenly down on his backside again. Stunned bystanders broke into spontaneous laughter and ironic applause and Tom, giving up the struggle to get back on his feet, let his natural showmanship trump his embarrassment, and doffed his hat to acknowledge them.

David Payne came running to the edge of the ice. "I got that! Wonderful. Well done, Tom! That wasn't what I had in mind, but it couldn't have gone better if we'd rehearsed all day."

Tom crawled across to the safety of the bank. "I didn't do it on purpose," he said.

"Never mind that," said Payne. "With a bit of luck, we might have something to sell to the newsreels. They're always looking for a laugh to lighten the gloom. Let's get a few more shots of people who know what they're doing, then if it all comes out of the bath OK, we'll suggest that they run it with your bit at the end."

"But we've got to leave for Manitoba in the morning."

"I know. That can't be helped, but we can leave all this footage with a friend of mine in Quebec City. He works for the Edison network. I can trust him to pass on the money if they buy it. And don't worry, I'll make sure you get your share."

"Edison?" said Tom, "I know him. Or rather, my Dad does, and his friend Doctor Farcett. They worked together on the X-Ray."

Payne remembered how Pop and Billy had warned him about Tom's fantastic stories. He sighed as he heaved the tripod onto Tom's back, and they set off for a new vantage point.

"No, really," said Tom, "it's true." His voice cracked as he thought again of all the adventures he had lived through with Montmorency and Farcett.

"You're very convincing," said Payne. "You should be an actor. Maybe even a comedian if that little episode looks as funny on film as it did in real life. *Tom Evans: heaven sent to make you laugh.* There's no reason why we shouldn't have comedy stars at the movies, just like we do in the theatre. But you'd need a new name. Tom Evans is too plain. Thomas Evans doesn't sound right. You should go for something more fancy. You could take a place name. What about this place? Tom Montmorency. Thomas Montmorency. Now that sounds pretty unusual."

Tom could see this was no moment to talk about the coincidence of the waterfall bearing a name he not only recognised, but felt perfectly entitled to use. It would only add to the picture Pop and Billy had painted of a hopeless liar. In any case, if he didn't want to be found, the last thing he should do is get himself advertised under Montmorency's name. He tried to divert Payne with talk of other places: "There's Paterson," he said, "or we met at Fort Lee. Tom Lee?"

"That's just as bad as Tom Evans. Tom Fort? Thomas Fort? It's still much too plain. No, Montmorency is better…"

Tom interrupted, still trying to steer Payne from the M word: "I was born on a Scottish island called Tarimond. How about that?"

"Tom Tarimond," Payne repeated it a few times. "Tom Tarimond… Thomas Tarimond… Yes, I like the sound of that. I'll get my friend to add it to the title of our little waterfall film: *Introducing Thomas Tarimond.* We might as well give it a whirl."

Tom's memory lurched to images of Fregoli cavorting in front of his adoring fans. "Yes. I like it too. Thomas Tarimond it is."

"Just remember me when you're rich and famous!" laughed Payne. "And in the meantime, don't forget I'm your boss. Come on. Let's get some more work done before it gets dark."

As Tom carried the tripod across the icy bank, thoughts of stardom started to slip away. His muscles would remind him of his accidental performance at Montmorency Falls for some days to come.

23. Another Letter

Sunday came and went, and neither Malpensa nor any Italian clowns had arrived in town. Montmorency had to admit to himself that his fixation on the word *Domenica* which he had heard so often in connection with *Lo* Zoppo must have been misplaced. He remembered Farcett's reference to *Doppo*, and looked that word up in Tom's dictionary. At first he couldn't find it, and he began to wonder whether Farcett might be right about *Zoppo and Doppo*, the pair of comedians, but there it was, a bit higher up the page, with only one 'p'. *Dopo* : afterwards, later, subsequent. So the workmen might have been talking about next Sunday, the day of the parade Mary was helping to organise. Montmorency could hardly bear it: another week to wait.

On Tuesday morning, Montmorency went through his usual routine of eating Tom's breakfast upstairs, wetting Tom's tooth-brush in the bathroom, and then arriving late in the dining room to force down a little more food.

Frank was alone there, standing at the window. "How's Tom today?" he asked, without turning round.

Montmorency shrugged, "Oh, you know. No change," he said, and made his way over to the sideboard.

"I got a letter this morning," said Frank. "It's there on the table. Take a look if you like. You'll know who it's from as soon as you see the handwriting on the envelope."

Montmorency picked up the letter, half expecting to see a loopy Italian script. Maybe Malpensa had found him at last, and this was some teasing threat. Yet Frank seemed unconcerned, and the address on the envelope was unremarkable. The characters were round and evenly formed. Montmorency had no idea who could have sent the letter.

"I haven't a clue whose writing this is. May I read it?"

Frank turned around. "You don't recognise the way he crosses his *t*s so high up?" he said, still calm. "You haven't seen that long tail on the *y* before?"

Montmorency looked more closely at the address, bemused. He had never seen Armitage's writing. Was this some new twist in his plan? *I should get a grip on myself*, thought Montmorency, *it's probably something totally innocuous. Could it be from Harrison Bayfield? Maybe it's a simple thank you from someone we've helped at the soup kitchen.*

"What about the *S*? See the way it slants. Familiar?"

Before Montmorency could answer, Frank lunged at him, suddenly furious, seizing him by the lapels. "Good God, man! What kind of father are you? You don't even know what his handwriting looks like!"

"Tom?" gasped Montmorency, barely interrupting Frank's flow.

"What the devil's going on, man? He's in Canada. Why on earth have you been pretending to us that he's in his room upstairs?"

Montmorency didn't know where to begin. "I can explain," he said, trying to free himself from Frank's grip, so that he could read the letter, his heart bursting with relief at this sign that Tom was still alive, and with terror at the thought of revealing the deception to Frank.

"Explain? How on earth can you explain? It's clear from what he says that he didn't tell you where he was going, and that he's been gone since the day Fregoli left. All that time you've been pretending that he's upstairs, sulking in his room, when we could have been out there looking for him. Why? What possible explanation can there be for that?"

Montmorency stuttered, "It's complicated."

"You're too damn right it is!" said Frank, his face so close that his spittle hit Montmorency in the eye. "And what if you'd seen the letter first? What if you had guessed who it was from? What would you have done then, eh? Hidden it away? Carried on with your subterfuge? Let us all hate Tom for the way his childish temper has been dragging us all down, when in fact he's out there, alone, facing who-knows-what dangers? He's your son, for goodness' sake. How could you do this?"

"I told you. I have my reasons."

"Oh, I bet you do! And I dare say they're pretty selfish – or yet another concoctions of lies. That's what you do best, isn't it? Deceit. It's your speciality! Well, I don't want to hear any more of your excuses. I wouldn't believe them anyway."

Frank's hand moved up to grip Montmorency's throat, and with the other he tore Montmorency's wallet from his top pocket.

"I'm going after him. I'm taking every penny you've got in here, and I'm going to find him, and show him that somebody cares!"

"I'll come too!" Montmorency tried to shout, but Frank's grip tightened.

"Don't you dare! I'm doing this alone. I never want to see you again. And if you read that letter, you'll see that Tom feels the same way!"

Montmorency tried to pull Frank's hand from his windpipe, but the younger man was stronger, and in any case, Montmorency didn't want to hurt his friend. He could understand his rage and contempt. He even shared them. Frank pushed Montmorency to the ground, kicked him in the belly, and in a moment he was gone. Montmorency, gasping for breath, pulled himself up to the windowsill, hoping he would be able to see where Frank was going. He was too late. He staggered to the stairs, praying that Doctor Farcett wouldn't appear and ask what all the shouting was about. Then he shut himself in Tom's room, and sat down on the bed to read his letter.

Dear Frank,

Maybe you are angry with me for leaving without saying goodbye, but I had to move quickly to stand any chance of catching up with Fregoli, and anyway I didn't want you to talk me out of going. Just in case you have been worrying about me, this is to let you know that I am safe. But I am not coming back to Paterson. Fregoli had sailed before I could reach New York, but I have met a man who makes movies, and he is letting me help him with his work. It's really exciting. We are on our way to Quebec in Canada, and we're going to travel westwards – filming as we go. I'm not sure exactly where I'll be, but it will be a long way from Montmorency, and that is the most important thing for me. I can't bring myself to call him Dad any more. I will never understand why he stopped me going away with Fregoli, but maybe now he will realise how much it meant to me to follow him.

Tell him I'm sorry that I stole his money. I was in a hurry, and I took much more than I meant to. I am being paid now, and I will save up to pay him back one day, should we ever meet again.

Please give my love to Mary, and Robert. I am sorry for any distress I have caused them.

Tom

Montmorency's relief that Tom was safe was overwhelmed by his agony at the coldness of the letter. He was hurt that Tom thought he would be more upset about his missing money than his lost son, and he couldn't fail to notice that Tom sent love to the others – even to Mary – but not to him. It was clear that Tom knew his disappearance would have caused distress to Frank, but he either assumed that Montmorency was suffering no agony, or took pleasure in increasing it by deliberately denying him any kind words.

Montmorency ached to get away and chase after Tom, just as Frank had done. He longed to be able to tell Tom how he was only trying to keep everyone safe. He wished he had been able to find a way to explain to Frank that he had pretended Tom was still in Paterson to stop Armitage or Malpensa pursuing him. But he hadn't, and now the two young men Montmorency loved most both hated him. What's more, both of them were now on the loose, unknowing targets for a terrorist and the American secret service. Folding the letter, and slipping it into the pocket where his wallet had been, he returned to his own room, wondering how things could possibly get any worse. He opened the door.

Jerrold Armitage was sitting on his bed.

24. AN INVITATION

"I have to hand it to you, Montmorency," said Armitage. "You had us all fooled. We'd no idea that Tom had gone." Armitage looked down at a piece of paper in his hand, "I'm not surprised you look so dejected. It's pretty unforgiving, don't you think?"

Montmorency reached for his pocket, mystified at how Armitage had got hold of the letter so quickly.

"Oh, this is a copy," said Armitage, "The original was intercepted and re-sealed at the post office."

"What are you going to do to Tom?" asked Montmorency. "He's just a boy. He knows nothing of what is going on, or why I couldn't let him travel with Fregoli. He didn't know the danger he was putting himself in by running away."

"I understand that," said Armitage. "I'm not a complete monster, and anyway he's in Canada now. Our writ doesn't run there. We'll just have to hope that Malpensa doesn't get wind of where he is and chase up there to finish him off. If Tom has diverted him from our trap, there will be serious consequences for you all."

"Or those of us who are still here. Frank's left too now, you know."

"Oh, we know, all right," said Armitage. "But I think you'll find that he hasn't got far. We've got to make sure that everyone is in place for when Malpensa arrives."

"So you still expect Malpensa to come here?"

"Yes, and it won't be long now."

"Is that why you're here?" said Montmorency. "You're not usually in the thick of things."

"I won't take that as the insult that was, no doubt, intended," Armitage took a stiff white card from his briefcase. "Among other things, I came to give you this." He passed over the card. It was a hand-written with ornate lettering. "It's a grateful invitation from the city fathers of Paterson. They want you and Frank to ride at the head of the procession to the rededication of the church on Sunday."

Montmorency sneered. "And this was all their idea?"

"Let's just say it's been pointed out to the Mayor that it would do wonders for Anglo-American relations if there were to be some formal pubic recognition of your heroism on the night of the fire, and your hard work for the homeless."

"And they asked you to deliver the invitation personally?"

"The desk clerk kindly let me have it on my way up."

"As he slipped you the key to my room, I suppose? No doubt he feels unable to deny anything to his real boss."

Armitage said nothing, but shrugged.

Montmorency continued. "You're hanging us out like flags, aren't you – as a target for Malpensa. You think he's going to be there, at the ceremony?"

"We have our suspicions. You might be able to firm them up into something more substantial. That's the real reason I'm here."

Armitage took a stack of paper from his bag. He shuffled the sheets lazily, as if preparing to show them off one by one, knowing that Montmorency wouldn't be able to resist sneaking a look. Each page bore a drawing of a face.

"These are artists' impressions of suspicious characters seen in the vicinity," he said.

Armitage had feared that Montmorency might try to trick him – deliberately identifying the wrong man, so that he could get to Malpensa first – but, as he'd hoped, Montmorency's whole body betrayed recognition when Malpensa's face came to the top of the pack. "That's him?"

"Yes." Montmorency had no doubt.

"He was seen in Trenton yesterday," said Armitage. "It's just a short train ride away. He may be in town already."

"You lost him?"

"His whereabouts now are no business of yours. We just wanted to make sure we're on to the right man. I've got what I came for."

Montmorency stood in the way of the door, barring Armitage's way out. "No business of mine! The man wants to kill me! Tell me where he is. I need to get to him first!"

"You will do no such thing. Don't you dare deviate one jot from my instructions. We want him alive. We need to break him to see what plans the anarchists are hatching. The whole point of our mission is to protect the President."

"You won't break Malpensa. He won't talk."

"Oh, we'll find a way. Believe me, he's weak, just like all demagogues. They write, and make speeches urging others on to their deaths, but they never risk their own skins. He'll give way under pressure."

"Torture, you mean?" said Montmorency.

"Let's call it 'enhanced interrogation'."

"And you'll believe what he says when he's in agony?"

"Look, if only a fraction of what he says is true, it might save a life."

"And if it isn't, you may end up wasting your time on false leads – maybe imprisoning or killing innocent people," said Montmorency. "It's no way to behave."

"Oh, spare me your British chivalry!"

"What about The Rule of Law? Isn't that American enough for you?"

"That's precisely what I am seeking to defend!" said Armitage.

"Defend it by suspending it?" Montmorency sniffed. "You're seeking promotion, more like. You're just looking for a result at any price. And where are you going to be on the day of the parade? Up in the front with me – a perfect target?" Armitage said nothing. Montmorency couldn't contain his contempt. "I thought not. You don't put yourself in the front line any more than those demagogues do. You'll be lurking somewhere comfortable, co-ordinating things, staying out of danger, ready to take the credit while I'm on display like a duck in a shooting range, and your brave men are scattered through the crowd waiting to pounce on Malpensa if he takes a pop at me."

"You might be lucky," said Armitage. "Malpensa's courage could fail, or he might aim at Frank first. We've had every possibility covered since this mission began – except for losing Tom, of course. That's one up to your side."

"But we're supposed to be on the same side!"

"Of course." Armitage composed himself. "A slip of the tongue. And who knows, things may turn out in the best possible way. We may find Malpensa in the crowd before he has a chance to shoot. If all goes well, we will save your life." Armitage took another piece of paper from his pocket. "You do want to live, don't you?" he asked as his eyes scanned this new letter. "To survive, so you can get away from here and go to Scotland, to London, or to Florence with your friends the Duke and Duchess?"

"Where did you get that?" Montmorency asked, recognising the family letter he'd left on his desk awaiting a reply.

"Well, I had to find something to do while you and Frank were arguing downstairs. I've found interesting things on this desk before, remember. I've read and re-read that memoir of yours, by the way. I like your style. There's plenty in there that would be of interest to the authorities and the press on both sides of the Atlantic."

"I've told you before, I don't care what people think about me."

"But what about Frank, the Duke and Duchess or your rather intriguing friend, Vi Evans? Or dear, fragile, Doctor Farcett? Your medical authorities would take a dim view of some of his past activities, don't you think? One false move from you, and everything could be on the front pages of *The New York Times* and the *The Times* of London. You may have noticed that I have contacts in the press?"

Montmorency snorted with disdain. Armitage plucked a newspaper from the waste basket. It bore yet another photograph of Montmorency at work in the soup kitchen, with an invented quote about how sad he was to have failed to rescue Moretti, the librarian, from the fire.

"I knew you must have put that in," said Montmorency. "Just in case Malpensa needed tickling up. To remind him that I killed his henchman. A man who – may I remind you – you and all your so-called intelligence officers insisted was a simple Italian immigrant, trying to do the best for himself. We knew that he was really Moretti, that he'd killed George, and that he probably had a hand in the assassination of King Umberto too. So much for your fancy American intelligence service! And now you're advocating torture and barbarism."

Armitage turned the pages of the newspaper, and pointed to another report. "If you're talking about barbarism, I think it's you British who take the palm," he said. "What about your concentration camps in South Africa? Thousands of people have lost their homes, and are dying in the cause of your pointless war against the Boers. Don't give me lectures about good behaviour. If you ask me, any British cause for pride died with Queen Victoria."

"That's completely irrelevant," said Montmorency.

But Armitage pressed on. He put his hand on Montmorency's shoulder and his tone became friendlier, if a little patronising. "You're a man that citizens of Britain and America might be proud of. Go through with this, and no one need ever know about your past. Whatever happens on Sunday, you will be covered in glory, dead or alive. That's why Saturday's paper will have a full diagram of the rededication procession, showing how you and Frank will be right beside the Mayor at in the parade, and on the platform for the speeches. Let's hope Malpensa buys a copy."

"And shoots at me. Why do you hate me so much?"

"I don't hate you. I have no personal feelings about you at all." Armitage shrugged. "Well, to be honest, I do harbour a little irritation at the professional bother you dropped me in when you let me down at Buffalo…" Montmorency tried, unsuccessfully to interject with an explanation. "…And of course you represent a nation that roughed-up and disabled a valued colleague…"

"Who was operating undercover on our soil without permission," Montmorency said.

"Be careful, you're getting close to justifying what you criticise."

"But what happened to Miles Beck was an accident – a misunderstanding. Your use of me is planned. And in any case, the mistake in Britain was nothing to do with me. I was nowhere near. You can't make me the whipping boy."

"You're no scapegoat," said Armitage. "You're a vital means to an end. I'm sorry your role in all this isn't more glamorous for you. And believe me, we don't want you to die. We just accept that it's a possibility. If you survive on Sunday, you will be free to go. In fact we would like you to. If you're killed, we will give you a splendid funeral. You will be painted rosy – very rosy indeed. A hero. The only downside is that you won't be here to see it."

Armitage made for the door again. Montmorency was torn about whether to mention what he'd heard about *Lo Zoppo*, and how that might be a codename for Malpensa.

"Let me out." Armitage commanded. "I'll see you on Sunday at the parade. You won't see me, but I'll be there."

"Just one more thing," said Montmorency. "There's a name I've been hearing around the town. *Lo Zop…*"

"*Zoppo*," said Armitage. "Yes, we know all about him. We have a very good informant."

Montmorency's mind went back to Farcett's missing notes. Once again he found himself wondering exactly how his friend fitted in to all this. But then a commotion downstairs sent them both lurching to look out of the bedroom window. Armitage got there first, and blocked Montmorency's view. Someone was thumping on the front door of the hotel. The bellboy was frantically calling for Montmorency, and for Doctor Farcett, too.

"I think you'd better go down," said Armitage, and Montmorency got to the lobby just as Farcett was emerging from the smoking room. Slumped across the doorway lay Frank, unconscious and badly beaten up.

Farcett sent Montmorency back upstairs for his medical bag. Montmorency took the chance to look into his own room. Jerrold Armitage had gone – no doubt to congratulate the agents who had stopped Frank leaving town.

25. PREPARATIONS

It wasn't the first time Montmorency had cradled Frank's bruised and battered body through a long night. It was the first time he had done it with a burning lie in his heart. He didn't want to tell Frank about Malpensa. He knew that, if he did, Frank would ignore his injuries and put all his might into slaying the mastermind of his uncle's murder. Dazed by painkillers, Frank lay on a daybed specially set up in the smoking room to save him from having to climb the stairs. His wild mixture of rage and incoherent questions was taken by Doctor Farcett as an understandable response to the attack and the drugs.

But, upstairs, the doctor was troubled. Frank had rambled about Tom being lost, and so Farcett had tried Tom's door, only to find that it was unlocked, and that Tom was not inside. He pieced together the jigsaw of information he had gathered through the day, and decided that Frank must have run after Tom to the train station and been attacked before he could stop the boy from getting away. Farcett wondered whether Montmorency knew that Tom had gone, and decided to go down to break the news gently.

It was late, but Montmorency was still awake. Standing in the doorway of the smoking room, Farcett could see that Montmorency, sitting beside Frank's bed, was quietly sobbing. This was no time for a confrontation or for breaking bad news. Perhaps Montmorency already knew that Tom had run away, and longed to seek him out, but felt he could not leave this other young man, groaning in drug-induced sleep after a savage beating.

Farcett was about to go when Montmorency spoke.

"Robert. Is that you?"

"I'll take over for a bit," said Farcett. "You need to sleep."

"I suppose I do. But before I go, perhaps we'd better talk about Tom?" said Montmorency, who thought Farcett had known about Tom's flight days ago. "Do you think I should have gone after him?"

"Well, there's no way you can know where he is," said Farcett, unaware of the letter from Canada. "I know it must be heartbreaking for you, but I'd say you can probably do more good staying here, and looking after Frank. We can talk in the morning about how to search for Tom."

Frank's snoring grew louder, and Farcett went closer, to make sure that nothing was wrong. "It's the sleeping draught," he said. "We won't get any sense out of him until tomorrow. Go to bed, Montmorency. We'll discuss all this properly when you've had a decent rest."

Montmorency wanted to talk some more, but he heard the night porter shuffling along the corridor outside the room. Once again he mentally congratulated Farcett on managing to construct an apparently anodyne conversation when they might be overheard.

"I'll try to get some shut-eye," Montmorency said. "But please wake me if there are any developments."

Montmorency didn't sleep well, but by dawn he had decided to use the attack to keep Frank out of danger at the parade.

When Mary arrived at the hotel next morning – full of shocked concern, and offering to sit with Frank while Montmorency manned the soup kitchen – she agreed that it would be best if Frank declined the Mayor's invitation for the sake of his health.

"I'll go and tell him," she said.

Frank was groggy, but able to conduct a proper conversation for the first time since the attack. He was only too happy to miss the event. "I hate that kind of thing," he said. "Those thugs have done me a favour if it means I don't have to dress up and listen to speeches."

"A high price to pay for that," said Mary, as she plumped his pillows, and straightened the counterpane. "Why do you think they attacked you?"

"I was outside the railway station. They must have thought I had enough money for a train ticket, at least. I was angry. I didn't have my wits about me. I wasn't looking out for myself."

"What were you angry about?" asked Mary.

"Hasn't Montmorency told you? Good God! Is there no end to the man's duplicity? It's Tom. Don't you know he's in Canada? He ran away on the day Fregoli left. Montmorency's been lying to us all about the big sulk. I was on my way to look for Tom. I can't believe that Montmorency hasn't explained all that to you."

Mary tried to disguise her surprise and the hurt she felt about being kept in the dark. "We haven't really had a chance to talk," she said, changing the subject back to the assault on Frank. "You've been the centre of attention, you know. I can only apologise for the behaviour of my fellow citizens." Montmorency came into the room as she was speaking, looking for his overcoat so that he could leave for the soup kitchen. Forgetting for a moment that she had never told Montmorency of her misfortune, Mary carried on talking to Frank, "They attacked me, remember. Some people have been quite desperate and undisciplined since the fire."

"Have you seen my coat?" said Montmorency, as Mary simultaneously realised her error and faced the blow of Montmorency's apparent indifference to the news that she had been assaulted. She couldn't bring herself to believe Frank's story that Montmorency had lied about Tom. And in the midst of all that, she was waiting for Montmorency to offer her Frank's place alongside him at the parade.

As Montmorency fastened his buttons, she even dropped a hint. "Would you like me to tell the committee that Frank can't take part in the rededication?" she said.

"Oh, yes please," said Montmorency. "I haven't really got time to write."

Mary left a beat of time for Montmorency to invite her to ride alongside him in Frank's place. There was only a silence, which she filled. "Perhaps Frank could go up to Harrison's house to watch from there. Harrison's nerves are too frayed for him to join in a public celebration."

"That's a good idea," said Montmorency, without lifting his eyes as he pulled on his gloves. "Could you sort that out with Bayfield? I'm sure they'll enjoy each other's company – and yours too. It would be wonderful if you could be there to make sure that Frank doesn't overdo things. Indeed, I'm not sure Frank should go at all unless you're there to nurse him." He looked at the clock. "Good heavens, is that the time? I'd better be on my way."

Montmorency strode from the room without another glance at Frank or Mary. He didn't want to give either of them the chance to argue against his plan. He was happy that they would both be in a safe place on Sunday. He knew that Frank was still furious about Tom, and determined to go searching for him as soon as he had the strength. He didn't know that Mary was mystified as to why Montmorency, so obviously desperate to get her out of his way on Rededication Day, no longer seemed to care for her.

26. REDEDICATION
DAY I

On the night before the parade, Montmorency, Frank and Farcett had a quiet supper together. Montmorency was tempted to hint to the doctor that he understood the dangers he must face in the morning, but he didn't want to risk giving Frank any inkling that something was up. Montmorency couldn't turn his mind to any other subject, but he tried to sound unconcerned, even casual.

"So, Robert, are you going to watch the procession from the Bayfield house, too?"

"I'll take Frank up there, of course," said the doctor. "I'll try to make sure he doesn't get bounced around too much on the way. Those bruises must still be pretty sore."

"You're telling me!" said Frank, as Farcett continued.

"But then I think I'll go down into town for the parade itself. They always need medics on hand at that kind of event. People faint in the heat or the cold, or trip up in the crush. And anyway, if I mingle with the crowd, I might pick up some useful stuff for my psychological study. This could be the moment when the people of Paterson make the transition from collective victimhood to a feeling of hope. I wouldn't want to miss it."

To Montmorency's ears, the doctor's explanation seemed too full. His suspicions of his old friend returned. Was he really intending to be there because he knew Malpensa was coming?

Was he planning to be on hand in case Montmorency was injured? Or was he under instructions from Armitage to make sure that Montmorency stayed in place as a lure and target for Malpensa, so that his agents could catch the Italian, and take the credit for foiling an anarchist plot against the President?

Montmorency ached for a proper conversation with Farcett, to explain his own recent behaviour, and to take his leave, in case this was their last night together, but he so feared confirmation that Farcett was conspiring to risk his death that he chose to say nothing more. Instead, he went upstairs and packed his belongings, either for a quick getaway if he survived the parade, or to make things easier for Mary, Frank and Robert if he did not. He knew he wouldn't sleep, so he stayed up, writing an account of what he had been doing in Paterson, explaining how Armitage had trapped him; how he had never meant to hurt or disappoint anyone, but had striven to ensure the safety of those he loved most, especially Mary, whose forgiveness and understanding he implored, adding a new proposal of marriage, with a promise of eternal devotion. He sealed the envelope, addressed to Mary, and slid it into his valise, ready to show it to her in person if he survived, and hoping someone would post it to her if he did not.

In the morning, Montmorency took a long and fragrant bath, trimming his toe and finger nails, and taking special care as he shaved. It was a long time since he had worn his best clothes: a fine cotton shirt fastened with studs and cufflinks that had once belonged to his friend Lord George Fox-Selwyn; a soft silk cravat, bought in the first, happy, days of their trip to Florence in search of stolen museum exhibits; a brocade waistcoat from Paris; and a heavy tail coat, made by the elderly London craftsman who had tended to him since his first days as a gentleman. He couldn't decide between a new silk topper from Manhattan, and his original folding opera hat, which he somehow believed might bring him luck. It was still too early for breakfast. He sat on his bed, playing with the mechanism. *Thwhopp, thwhopp, thwhopp.*

Eventually, he decided to go downstairs, to make sure he said a proper goodbye to Frank. The daybed was surrounded by bottles of medicine and liquor, and Frank was snoring heavily. It seemed a shame to rouse him after what had clearly been a troubled, painful night. Montmorency leaned over and brushed Frank's forehead with a kiss – not enough to wake him, but for Montmorency an unusually physical expression of affection, even love, for the young man who had shared so many of his adventures, and been part of the nearest thing to family that Montmorency had ever known.

Doctor Farcett came down, and agreed that Frank should be allowed to sleep until it was time to leave for the Bayfield house.

"I'd better set off before you," said Montmorency.

"Yes, but you've time for some breakfast first," said Farcett. "You don't want to spend a morning in the cold with nothing inside you. Let's go through."

They went into the dining room, where the usual lavish buffet was laid out. Farcett helped himself with gusto. Montmorency was amazed, even a little offended, by Robert's capacity for relaxation as the denouement of the drama through which they had been living drew near. He scooped a random selection of food onto his own plate, knowing he would only pick at it, even though he was no longer eating for Tom. He and Robert were alone. Montmorency knew that this might be his last chance to talk to the man who had saved his life, helped him reinvent himself, and shared the fun and peril of more than two decades. Should he try to put his gratitude into words, or take the chance to find out exactly where the doctor stood in this latest, perhaps last, predicament? Whose side was he really on? And if not Montmorency's, why not? Montmorency looked around. There were no servants on hand. It seemed that, at last, he and Farcett were truly alone.

"Robert," he said. "There's something I want to ask you. It's been so hard, not being able to talk openly these past few weeks, but surely today we can clear the air."

Farcett looked up from his breakfast, slightly bemused.

"I just need to know," said Montmorency, faltering. "And to explain to you…"

The door opened, and a portly stranger in clerical robes walked in.

"Good morning, gentlemen," he said breezily. "Do you mind if I join you?" He didn't wait for an answer, and poured himself some coffee. Settling at the table, he introduced himself. "Martin Greenshaw. I'm here to represent the episcopal congregations of Manhattan at the rededication of the church. Got in last night. I must say, they do a fine breakfast here!"

Montmorency and Farcett greeted the clergyman politely, and the conversation turned to the fire, the reconstruction of Paterson, and the events of the day ahead.

After half an hour of idle chit-chat, Farcett looked at his watch. "You two had better be on your way, if you're going to join the parade before it sets off," he said.

"My goodness, is that the time?" said the Reverend Greenshaw. "Shall we meet in the lobby in five minutes, Mr Montmorency, and walk down together?"

"I'll go and see to Frank," said Farcett, leaving the room without even saying goodbye to Montmorency.

Before he knew it, Montmorency found himself walking towards the railway station, where the parade was to begin, only half listening to the clergyman chattering alongside him. The little round man was impressed by the effort the people of Paterson had made to decorate their town for the great event. Montmorency noticed that some of the home-made bunting featured fabrics donated to the soup kitchen by Harrison Bayfield. He wondered whether this was the best use for them, in the midst of winter, but he could see that the restoration of the church did, as Farcett had suggested, mark a real turning point for at least some of the townsfolk.

The Reverend Greenshaw was in no doubt that the project had been a good use of the skills of Paterson's best craftsmen, even when homelessness still blighted the town. "I can't wait to see what the builders have done," he said.

"I looked in the other day," said Montmorency. "It's plain – much less ornate than the church that burnt down – but I think it's rather beautiful. There are new hangings, woven at the silkworks – so at least some jobs came out of the project. And there's a very fine stained-glass window, showing a phoenix rising from the ashes."

Montmorency didn't mention that the window had been donated by Harrison Bayfield in the immediate aftermath of the fire, before he had realised the true extent of his own financial disaster. He had not felt able to withdraw the offer, and his bank had been too embarrassed to bounce a cheque made out to the church, but Montmorency had no doubt that their lawyers would be working on ways of getting the money back if Harrison Bayfield died, or his estate had to be sold.

"The window was the gift of the man who lives in that house," said Montmorency, pointing up to the Bayfield mansion high above the town. He felt a sudden desire to protect the jovial clergyman from the bloodbath that might lie ahead. "You'd get a fine view of the parade from there, you know," he said. "I'm sure Doctor

Farcett would be happy to introduce you to Harrison Bayfield. He's entertaining a small group for the occasion. Perhaps that would be your best vantage point."

"Oh no," said Greenshaw. "I really must take part in the parade, and in the service in the church. It's my duty."

"Of course," said Montmorency, knowing that what Greenshaw said must be right, but unable to stop himself wondering whether he really was a minister, or whether the duty of which he spoke was to make sure that Montmorency was in place, and a prominent target, at the commemoration. Was he yet another of Armitage's men?

Back at the hotel, Frank was slowly, and painfully, getting dressed, cursing the robbers who had beaten him up. Through his hangover, a question niggled. If the attackers were only after his money, why had they crossed Paterson to dump his body on the hotel step? Had it really been a simple robbery, or was someone warning him not to leave town? Why would they do that? He set off for breakfast, his injured leg dragging behind him. *Just like Malpensa*, he thought, at first jokingly, but then with a rising mixture of panic and excitement. Images from the past flashed into his brain: His first sight of the injured anarchist three years ago in Milan, where Montmorency had taken him to see an opera; the master strategist addressing a secret meeting in London; fleeing from him through the streets of Paris. Another connection was slowly coupling. *Lo Zoppo*. Until now, Frank had paid little attention to Farcett's mentions of the Italian clown who was due to visit any day. He'd half recognised the name, and assumed that he must have heard of him when he lived in Florence, or perhaps this was one of the many rival showmen

Fregoli had denigrated in late-night, drunken anecdotes. But now he put the clues together, just as Montmorency had done long before. Defying his pain, he dragged himself upstairs, and, like Montmorency, made for Tom's Italian-English dictionary. *Lo Zoppo*: the limping one. Malpensa must be on his way.

Frank burst back onto the landing, determined now to get down to the parade. He ran straight into Doctor Farcett.

"Frank! What on earth are you doing up here? You really shouldn't be exerting yourself climbing the stairs!"

"You're right," said Frank, thinking quickly of a way to get out of accompanying Farcett to the Bayfield house. "I should have known better. I thought I ought to have a proper bath, but I've overdone it. I'm not sure I'm up to travelling across town now. You go without me, please."

Frank looked so agitated and short of breath that the doctor was easily convinced. "Well, now you're up here, you might as well lie down in your own bed. Lean on my arm, and I'll get you settled."

"Thanks," said Frank. "Do apologise to Mary and Mr Bayfield for me."

"I'm sure they'll understand," said Farcett. "You stay here, and concentrate on getting well."

"I will," said Frank, waiting only for Farcett to leave the hotel before setting off for the parade himself.

It seemed an age before the doctor shouted a farewell and climbed into the carriage that had been hired to take Frank up, past the waterfall, to the Bayfield mansion. When the sound of the horses' hooves had died away, Frank looked round the room for something he could use as weapon. In the end, he had to improvise, putting a heavy paperweight into a sock to make a cosh. It wasn't much, but it made him feel a little safer, and he was fully prepared to use it aggressively if it meant he could wipe out the man who had ordered the death of his Uncle George. Leaning on the bannister for support, he half-walked, half-slid his way downstairs and made for the hallstand. But as he reached up for his coat, a hand came across his mouth, and in a haze of acrid fumes he slumped, unconscious, to the ground.

27. MANITOBA

In Canada, Tom was helping to prepare lunch for ten: Mr and Mrs Freebody, six of their noisy children, himself and Davy Payne. The seventh child, a newborn boy, was sleeping in a basket by the fire. Tom and Davy had spent a hectic few days travelling into the heart of the country, shooting footage of Canadian Pacific trains. Tom had learned how to set up the camera low at the rail-side so that audiences would scream in terror as mighty engines powered towards them through the cinema screen. He could time shots to reveal scenes of stupendous natural beauty as clouds of steam dispersed, and catch the urgent spinning of locomotives' wheels as they thundered from east to west and back again. At the end of each day, he put aside his job as camera assistant, and became Tom Tarimond, aspiring actor. Davy Payne would use a little precious film to catch Tom's slapstick performances – fruitlessly chasing animals and birds, falling over his own feet, and, in his most dramatic role so far, apparently rescuing a toddler from the railway track at the last minute (though this scene was shot using one of the Freebody children on a day when no trains were due, and the danger would have to be edited in later). But today was Sunday, and despite the wonderful light, Mrs Freebody considered it unseemly to assemble a tripod, or lace up a reel of film.

Tom was enjoying being part of a family, and the Freebodies drank in his stories of growing up in Tarimond, London, Europe and America, though they believed only a small proportion of what they heard. Tom loved the Canadian countryside, which seemed to him to be like Scotland seen through a magnifying glass, and his yearning to reconnect with Fregoli was eased by his excitement at being part of the Canadian Pacific filming project. He and Davy Payne had arrived in Manitoba with enough footage for Freebody to complete his new series of short movies designed to make people all over the world visit Canada as tourists or settlers, bringing their money and their skills with them. On their first night in the comfortable farmhouse on the outskirts of Winnipeg, Freebody had broken the news that he had persuaded Canadian Pacific to let Tom and Davy travel with him to England, to help him show the films in cinemas across the land. Everything was looking up.

The oldest child of the Freebody family was Rose, who, at thirteen, was both an aid and a trial to her mother. She would wash, dress and feed the little ones, keep an eye on them and run errands, but she was still a child herself, and could throw temper tantrums to rival two-year-old Bertie's. Today she was sulking, and in her moodiness, Tom found an uncomfortable reminder of his own behaviour back in Paterson.

"I couldn't possibly let you go," said Mrs Freebody, as she stirred the enormous stew pot on the kitchen range. "You're far too young."

"But Tom's going," said Rose. "He's not much older than me. You don't seem to mind about that."

"Tom's a boy, and he's got a job to do. And anyway, travelling to London will be taking him nearer home. I don't want you so far away from me. I'll need you here, with your Pa away. Especially now the baby's come."

"It's not fair," said Rose. "Why should Tom have all the fun?"

"It won't all be fun," said Mrs Freebody. "Touring can be hard work. Ask your father. His letters were nothing but a litany of moans last time."

"But I want to see other places, and meet new people. Just like Tom has."

"Well, give it time, and who knows – if your father's films bring in enough money, we might all go overseas one day. But for now, your place is with me and your brothers and sisters."

"You mean I'm your slave!" said Rose.

"Not a slave," said Mrs Freebody, clinging to what was left of her patience. "Just a member of the family, with all the responsibilities that brings."

"I never asked to be in this family."

"And we never asked for you, but we've got you." Mrs Freebody realised instantly how hurtful her slick remark was. "And we love you, and it would break my heart to be separated from you. I bet Tom's mother misses him,"

"My mother doesn't know I'm here," said Tom, not sure whether to support Rose or Mrs Freebody in the argument.

"What?" said Mrs Freebody, genuinely shocked. "Do you mean to say that you haven't written to say that you are safe?"

"I sent a letter to a friend in New Jersey," said Tom, as Davy Payne came into the room after a reluctant visit to church. "And he might be in touch with her. But I didn't tell him exactly where I was, and anyway I've moved on now. My mother is thousands and thousands of miles away. It would take an age for a letter to get from here to Tarimond,"

Mrs Freebody's attention shifted to Davy. "Where's my husband" she asked him.

"He's on his way. He just stopped off at the shed for a moment," said Payne.

"He's not working is he? For goodness' sake, it's Sunday, Davy! We have standards in this house, you know. We have rules."

Rose sniffed. "More for some than others," she moaned.

Davy Payne, sensing a build-up of tension between mother and daughter, and realising he might have landed his old friend in a spot of domestic trouble, steered the conversation back to the subject of Tom's letter. "Didn't you say you had a friend working at the British Embassy in Washington?" he asked, taking off his boots.

"Yes. What of it?" said Tom, guessing that Payne thought this was just another of his confabulations. "It's true, you know. He's the Marquess of Rosseley, but he's got a normal name too: Alexander Fox-Selwyn."

"Normal?" scoffed Rose.

Payne suppressed a smile. "Well, if he's really real, why not send the letter to him, to forward to your mother through diplomatic channels? It's bound to speed things up."

"She's staying with Alexander's father. He's the Duke of Monaburn," Tom said, realising from the look that passed between Payne and Mrs Freebody that his story was sounding more fantastic by the minute.

"Well then," said Davy Payne, indulgently, "she shouldn't be too hard to find."

Mrs Freebody wiped her hands on her apron. "Here, give me those carrots to peel, Tom, and you go off and write that letter. Tell your mother that you're safe and sound with us, and how my husband and Mr Payne will look after you all the way to London. I'm not going to pry into how and why you ended up here. But believe you me, your mother would give anything to know that you are alive and well. Find him a pen and paper, Rose, and make sure that he gets it written before lunchtime,"

Tom and Rose left the kitchen. Davy Payne reached for a carrot and took a bite. Mrs Freebody playfully slapped his wrist. "You can wait till they're cooked, like everyone else," she said, handing him a knife, "and lunch will be on the table all the sooner if you lend me a hand with the peeling and chopping."

They sat together at the table, working their way through the vegetables. Mrs Freebody couldn't disguise her concern for Tom. "How much do you know about him? Is he a runaway? Do you think his folks have any idea where he is?"

"Who knows whether the people he talks about really exist? The other day he started talking about someone called Montmorency, and we just happened to be at the Montmorency Falls. Maybe he just dreams up ideas as he goes along."

"And this Lord, Marquess, Duke, or whoever he is?"

"Well, it should be possible to check on him. He's supposed to be a British diplomat in Washington, and we'll get his name off the envelope. I'm going into Winnipeg tomorrow. I could send a cable. Or I could find the British Consul, and see if they can make contact with Washington. Who knows, they may even have a telephone. I might be able to talk to that double-barrelled gent of Tom's. I might even get the chance to read him the letter. Do you think I should?"

"I think it's a wonderful idea. But don't tell Tom. He trusts us, and we don't want him running away again."

"I'll go first thing in the morning. Get Mr Freebody to keep Tom here, helping out, and I'll take his letter into town. If all else fails, I can just post it in the normal way."

While they were talking, Tom – under Rose's stern gaze – wrote to Alexander, asking him to pass on his news to Vi in Scotland. He told of his work with the cinematographers, and how he would be helping out at a touring exhibition of their films in Britain very soon. He didn't mention his disappointment with, and anger towards, Montmorency, although he knew his mother would work out that something had gone terribly wrong. He understood that sending the letter probably meant an end to his plan to cut himself off from his family and friends forever, but as the smell of food filled the house, he found that he was truly happy for the first time in a very long while.

28. REDEDICATION
DAY 2

At Paterson station, a woman from the Ladies' Circle was checking the arriving dignitaries against a diagram showing the order of precedence in the procession. The parade was to be led by an open carriage. It was actually just a farmer's cart with benches strapped across the floorboards, decked out in red, white and blue. Montmorency confirmed that Frank would not be coming, and was relieved, as he squashed himself into place alongside the ample backside of the Mayor, that no one felt a need to find a replacement to join them in the front row of the cart. There was a slight hiatus while the band waited for their tuba player to join them, and the great and the good of Paterson, who were lined up to follow the cart, grew tired of standing still. Some stamped their feet to stop them from freezing. A few lit cigars and pipes. The town's Chief Engineer sloped off into the goods yard for a secret swig from his hip-flask, though it was only ten o'clock. Eventually, the missing musician arrived, running, full of apologies and a tale of an incontinent grandmother. As soon has he got his breath back and his music straight, he nodded to the drummer, who set the beat. The band stuck up *The Battle Hymn of the Republic*, and the cart lurched forward, jolting uncomfortably over ruts in the road.

Montmorency gazed around him, seeing murderers everywhere, but somehow managing to maintain a smile, and even remembering to return the waves of the jubilant crowd, which grew thicker as they approached the church. He spotted Farcett, making notes in his little book, and frantically scanned the throng for a limp, a cloak, and a wide-brimmed black hat, even though he knew that Malpensa would probably be in disguise, if he was there at all.

Twenty minutes and several stirring tunes later, they arrived at the church. The horses were detached from the cart, and the brakes applied, so that the Mayor could stand up in the cart, and make his speech in full view of the crowd. He had warned Montmorency that he would not spare his blushes when recounting to the people of Paterson all that their English visitors had done for the town during and after the fire. Montmorency was sweating, even though the weather was cold. The sun was bright, and low in the sky. He had to shield his eyes to look into the mass of people before him. It was hard to focus on individuals, but every other second Montmorency was conscious of movements and noises that might signal his end. A cloud passed over the sun. Faces were clearer now. There, straight ahead of him, was the doorman from the hotel. Was he one of Armitage's agents, there to protect him, and to look for Malpensa, or simply an interested citizen, out to witness an important event on his day off? Could he be part of Paterson's anarchist underground with a grudge against Montmorency for Moretti's death? The doorman reached inside his jacket. There was a flash, a bang, and a puff of smoke…

A photographer had taken a picture.

Everyone in the cart had been startled, but now they giggled at their momentary terror, and composed themselves, ready for another photo, more relaxed and smiling after the shock.

The Mayor rose to his feet, steadying himself with a hand on Montmorency's shoulder. He called on the padre from the church to join him in the cart to give a blessing to the crowd. The church was already full to overflowing, and there was no hope that any of them would get inside for the service. Everyone on the cart stood for the prayer. As the minister prefaced it with a few words about the fire – suggesting that it might have been a judgement on the past behaviour of Paterson's townsfolk – Montmorency spotted a man at the far left of his field of vision, taking a handkerchief out of his pocket. He remembered how President McKinley's assassin had used a napkin to hide his gun. He turned to look at the man. Could it be Malpensa? But he was bald and wiry and, as it turned out, he had a cold. He sneezed loudly into the cloth as the crowd muttered their *Amen*. Could that be a signal? But why would Malpensa need one? Montmorency was unprotected, and in full view of everyone: the most unmissable target Malpensa was ever likely to get.

With the blessing over, the photographer warned everyone to stand by, and there was another flash and bang. Then another – and the Mayor slumped into Montmorency's arms, crushing him down onto the bench under his weight. The pastor leaped to lend a hand, and the rest of the honour party dived under their benches, but – in an instant – the attention of the crowd was elsewhere: on a group of citizens sprayed with blood, and a body lying on the ground. After a moment's silence, someone screamed, and it was as if everyone had been given permission to shout, howl, and cry out. Montmorency saw Farcett forcing his way through to the casualty. Men with guns were doing the same, coming forward from all directions. Montmorency recognised several of them: the postman, the shopkeeper from the drug store, a station clerk, the hotel chef. Armitage's men, no doubt, breaking cover at last. If Mary had been alongside Montmorency in the cart, she would have recognised the tall, muscular figure who reached up to pull the Mayor from the carriage and into the church. It was the stranger who had rescued her from the two young thieves. Two more men grabbed Montmorency and manhandled him through the church porch to the spot where the Mayor was lying, unconscious. Who were these people? Agents of the state, or disciples of Malpensa?

The organist was still playing, unaware of the drama outside, and assuming that the pastor and his honoured guests were simply making rather a commotion as they arrived for the service. Montmorency and the men who had brought him inside tore off the Mayor's outer clothes to get at his wounds. But there was no sign of blood, and after a few moments the Mayor's huge body began to stir. He was alive, and uninjured. He must have fainted at the sound of the shot in the crowd, or even just the pop of the photographer's flash gun. A few parishioners at the back of the church had turned round to see what was going on. They could barely disguise the mixture of disappointment and contempt they felt at the sight of the fat official trying to regain his dignity after the alarm.

All Montmorency wanted to do now was to find out who had been hit in the crowd, and who had pulled the trigger. He tried to get out of the church, but was held back by the men who had brought him there. Moments later, the door swung inwards, with Doctor Farcett supervising the delivery of a body covered by a coat. Montmorency recognised the garment as one donated to the soup kitchen by Harrison Bayfield. Would the victim turn out to be someone Montmorency had served with his ladle? Then he realised that one of the men carrying the body was in his shirtsleeves. He must have removed his coat to cover the victim's injuries from the gawping crowd.

When the coat was removed, Montmorency could see why. The wound was grotesque, and fatal. But the face, though contorted in the horror of its last moment, was recognisable. It was Malpensa or, as a voice from a pew behind him muttered, *Lo Zoppo*.

There could be no doubt, but Montmorency looked down to the corpse's legs to make sure. There was the damaged limb that had given Malpensa his distinctive limp. But there was no cloak, no broad-brimmed hat: none of the trappings that had helped give the anarchist his power over others. He was a diminished, lightweight figure in the checked shirt and workman's dungarees that had helped him blend in with the crowd. Yet this man had directed the assassination of kings and presidents. His mere existence had brought untold pain into Montmorency's own life. It was hard to believe that this small scrap of spent flesh could have instilled such fear, inspired acts of savage violence, and stripped one proud American, Jerrold Armitage, of the standards and values he purported to defend.

As Montmorency stood frozen, unable to look away, Farcett realised who the dead man was. "Oh dear God," he said. "Malpensa! What was he doing here?" After a moment's pause, he added, "He must have been aiming at you."

Montmorency was puzzled. "You mean you didn't know?"

"Know? Know what?"

His head spinning with the debris of weeks of fear and suspicion, Montmorency could only put his arm round his friend and mutter, "Oh, my dear Robert. We have a great deal to talk about."

One of the burly agents pulled at Montmorency's shoulder. "There'll be trouble at the factory when they hear about this. We'd better get you out of town quick."

The agent kicked the Mayor's coat out of the way and a bullet fell out of its folds, apparently stopped on its way to his heart by the Holy Bible in his pocket. He was to be a hero after all – the apparent target of a mad assassin from out of town.

Montmorency was buzzing with relief. He had survived Malpensa's final attempt on his life, and no one else had suffered, except the terrorist himself. And Armitage would be happy. A major threat to the life of President Roosevelt had been removed. Was it really all over at last? As he was bundled into a car at the back of the church, Montmorency could not stop a flood of hopeful tears.

29. THE GETAWAY

When they reached the hotel, the staff – many of whom Montmorency had spotted in the crowd at the parade – were already packing Robert Farcett's things. Frank was slumped, woozily, in a chair.

"We had to knock him out," said one of the agents. "He was a danger to the mission."

"What mission?" said Farcett, lifting Frank's wrist to feel his pulse.

"You tell me!" mumbled Frank.

Montmorency broke in sternly. "Just be thankful that you're both safe. I'll explain later. Get Frank on his feet, Robert. We're leaving. We've got to find Tom."

Montmorency ran up to his room. The valise he had packed the night before was on the bed, where he had left it, but when he opened it to make one last check that nothing was forgotten, he found the manuscript of his memoir lying on top. The other document, his explanation of his recent behaviour, had been removed. Armitage – away from the scene of the action as usual – had made one last visit.

An engine revved outside the window, and in minutes, with an escort of tough and silent agents, Farcett, Frank and Montmorency were forced into a car and on their way out of town. Montmorency begged them to stop at the Bayfield mansion so that he could see

Mary and tell her why he had not been himself for so long. He wanted to persuade her to join him in his search for Tom, or at least make arrangements for her to follow on as soon as possible. But the agents insisted, at gunpoint, that enough time had already been lost, and they were sped to a distant railway station, with tickets to Boston, and a sealed envelope to open on the train.

30. MOVING PICTURES

They had a carriage to themselves. *No accident*, thought Montmorency. *Armitage has everything organised.* Montmorency tried to explain his predicament in Paterson: why he had to do as Armitage insisted, for fear of endangering all their lives. He was flabbergasted to discover the extent of Farcett's ignorance of his plight. The doctor was not the splendid actor he had seemed, but an ignorant pawn in Armitage's great game. Frank opened the envelope. It contained three tickets for a transatlantic crossing the next day.

"We're not going to use them," said Montmorency. "If Armitage has agents waiting for us in Boston, we'll find a way to shake them off. We're going to look for someone who really can act. We're going to Canada to find Tom."

"It's one heck of a big country," said Frank. "How on earth are we going to track him down?"

"I don't know," said Montmorency. "But I won't stop till I do. He's my son. When we arrive in Boston, we'll find out how to get to Quebec. That's where he was going when he sent that letter."

"But he said he was moving on from there," said Frank.

Montmorency was angry for the first time since they'd left Paterson. "It's all we've got to go on, Frank. Please. Leave me with some hope!"

When their train pulled in to Boston, they had a surprise. They were on the alert for secret service men, but a familiar figure was waiting on the platform. It was Frank's brother – Alexander, Marquess of Rosseley.

Frank saw him first. "How did you know we would be here?" he asked.

"Armitage," said Montmorency, before Alexander could reply.

"Yes, but there's something else," said Alex. "Something Armitage doesn't know about. I'm taking you to a place where he can't touch you. To part of the British Empire. I've had some rather remarkable information from Manitoba in Canada."

"About Tom?" said Frank. "Did you know he's gone missing?"

"I didn't," said Alexander, with a note of irritation in his voice. "But I do now. And I know that he's about to set off for London, so I'm going to make sure that you all travel with him." Montmorency, Frank and Farcett all tried to interrupt with questions, but Alexander held up his hand to silence them. "I'll give you the full details later. We'll spend the night here, but first thing in the morning, we're setting off for Quebec to wait for him."

"And tonight we will tell you everything that's happened to us," said Frank. "You won't believe what's been going on. Malpensa…"

Alexander put a finger to his lips. "Stop, Frank. There will be a time and a place to talk, but a public railway station in foreign territory is not an appropriate spot. In any case, I think you'd be surprised at how much I already know." He gave Montmorency a conspiratorial glance, which was returned with an almost imperceptible nod.

"But may I ask," said Farcett, rather diffidently, "Your wife – Angelina?"

"Her pregnancy is progressing well, thank you, Robert," said Alexander, grateful for the chance to resort to social pleasantries, and back to his old booming voice. "Come on, I have a cab waiting. I think you'll find the hotel I have chosen rather more comfortable than the one in Paterson. And tomorrow we will set off north on our great adventure."

"Oh no," said Farcett. "No more adventures, please!"

31. WAITING IN QUEBEC

They went by ship. Montmorency, Farcett and Frank were all so exhausted that they spent much of the journey asleep, missing many spectacular sights along the way. But when they were awake, the food was good, and they arrived in Quebec refreshed, and longing to see Tom. Alexander went immediately to the offices of the Canadian Pacific Railway to discover what arrangements had been made for Freebody's British tour, and it turned out that they would have a week to wait before Tom and his new friends arrived in town. Davy Payne had warned Alexander that he thought Tom might run away again if he suspected that he was being lured into a trap, so it was decided that they should make no attempt to contact Tom before he reached Quebec.

Montmorency had written to Mary every day since they had left Paterson, desperately trying to explain what had happened, and why he had appeared so cold and distant in their last days together. He'd posted a letter at each stop along the way from Boston, giving the Post Office in Quebec as the return address, but when he got there, nothing was waiting for him. Five days later, he at last received a reply. It was friendly rather than loving; understanding rather than passionate. Much of it was taken up with an account of events in Paterson after the shooting. As the agent had predicted, Malpensa's death led to trouble at the silkworks. Harrison Bayfield's crumbling empire had taken yet another hit, and Mary was concerned for his mental, physical, and financial health. Harrison had reacted badly to losing Doctor Farcett's care so suddenly. She knew that Montmorency would understand that for her to leave too might push Bayfield to take actions none of them wished to contemplate, so joining Montmorency now was simply out of the question.

Montmorency understood her compassion. He loved and admired her all the more for her steadfast devotion to what she believed to be her duty. But he was hurt and surprised that she said nothing about his own predicament in Paterson. He wondered whether Armitage, as a final expression of power over Montmorency, was intercepting, and editing, his desperate attempts to contact and cosset the woman he adored.

When Montmorency replied to Mary's letter, explaining that he expected to accompany Tom to England any day now, he begged her to write to him at his London house, so that they could at last plan their future together. In the hope that Armitage had lost interest in him now that he was off American soil, he once again told the story of his reluctant role in the trapping of Malpensa, and why it had constrained his every word and deed. He promised her a new life with all that London had to offer an intelligent woman. Above all, he swore that their marriage would be free of politics, intrigue and deceit.

While they were waiting for Tom to arrive in Quebec, Farcett and Frank spent much of their time at a cinema near their hotel. It showed films distributed by the Edison company. On the first day, Frank had to stop Farcett giving a running commentary as a parade of the latest automobiles sped across the screen, and men panned for gold in a river.

"There's a good bit coming up," said Robert, as Frank dug him in the ribs.

"How do you know all that? Where have you seen these films before?" asked Frank as they left the theatre.

Robert recalled his night as a guest of Armitage in Edison's house in West Orange. Later, talking it through with Montmorency over a nightcap, he was persuaded that Armitage had never really been interested in his reports on the motivation of Paterson's discontented workers, useful though some of his incidental information on *Lo Zoppo* might have been. Farcett came to accept that he had been used as a weapon to keep Montmorency in line.

"Still," he said, "I've kept all my notes on my own psychological study. I've got some interesting points to make about how a community reacts to sudden trauma. I can go ahead and write my article, can't I?"

"I don't see why you shouldn't," said Montmorency, recognising the old, ambitious fire in Farcett's eyes. "And I hope it brings you the professional recognition you deserve."

Some of the newsreels at the cinema were quite old. They were shown time and time again. By the end of the week, Frank and Farcett knew them by heart. There was one from the previous September, about the assassination of President McKinley in Buffalo. It included the footage of McKinley's final speech that Armitage had shown to Farcett. Each time it came on the screen, Frank was transfixed by it, desperate to see whether he could spot himself, or McKinley's assassin, in the crowd. It was followed by scenes shot that same month showing a visit to Quebec by the Duke of York. Farcett wondered whether any of Armitage's men, or their Canadian counterparts, had been hidden among the cheering crowds that day, just in case of trouble. It was good to know that the Duke was safely home, and that a cinema on the far side of the Empire thought the film interesting enough to be shown months later.

One day, Frank and Farcett managed to persuade Montmorency to join them at the pictures, and afterwards they were all glad they'd gone. For after the usual fare that Montmorency had already been told so much about, there were two new features. The first was announced as *Winter Fun at Montmorency Falls*, and Frank and Farcett, sitting on either side of Montmorency, simultaneously nudged him when the familiar name came on screen. The film opened with people skating at the foot of a frozen waterfall. Then a young man was seen, trying to board a toboggan. He slipped, slid, and rolled his way down the slope, eventually giving up, and waving to the camera after his final failed attempt to stand. It was Tom, of course. They all recognised him, and in the dark cinema, as the rest of the audience howled with laughter, each of them allowed a tear to fall.

The next film was different from the others. Though still very short, it had more of a story to it. It was about a scruffy thief creeping up on a swaggering aristocrat to rob him. Both parts were played by Tom, in a showpiece of trick photography. The rich man was, to a tee, the younger Montmorency whom Frank and Farcett had both known. The vagabond was unmistakable to Montmorency and Farcett as Scarper, his original self, whose weaknesses had so often undermined his adopted status. There could be no doubt now about the identity of Tom's father. It was something Farcett had accepted, with regret, long ago, but the flimsy screen image somehow made the fact more real and solid. Knowing how desperate Montmorency was to make contact with Mary, and regretting his own missed opportunities in love, Farcett had been contemplating offering to accompany

Tom to London while Montmorency waited for his bride to be ready to leave North America. Now he realised that the most important thing was to keep father and son together. He only hoped that Tom and Mary would both be ready to travel soon.

32. BACK TO LONDON

As Freebody, Payne and Tom approached Quebec from Manitoba, communications became easier, and Davy Payne slipped off at stations along the way to send cables or make telephone contact with Montmorency. On Payne's advice, Montmorency and his friends waited until the ship had left harbour before revealing to Tom that they were on board. To everyone's surprise, he didn't respond with an angry outburst. There was real joy in his eyes when he saw his friends and, after accepting Montmorency's offer of a handshake, he let it fold naturally into a hug. By the time the ship docked at Liverpool after the long ocean voyage, everything had been explained, apologised for and forgiven. New resolutions and promises had been made on all sides.

When they arrived in London, they all stayed at Montmorency's club – Bargles – while his house was prepared for them. Frank's father and stepmother Gus and Beatrice, Duke and Duchess of Monaburn, were on their way south with Tom's mother, Vi Evans, so the first thing Montmorency did when they settled into Bargles was to arrange for a reunion dinner at the club. Montmorency had been hoping for a degree of anonymity in Britain, but it turned out that the staff at Bargles (all of whom were called Sam, for simplicity's sake) had cut out every article in *The New York Times* about his heroics in Paterson. The club always took a copy of that newspaper, even though it was at least a week old when it arrived. Armitage's extensive and glowing accounts of the wonderful English philanthropists were pinned on noticeboards in every corridor. Even Frank and Farcett were treated as celebrities in the bars (Big Drinks and Little Drinks). Montmorency was the toast of the two dining rooms (Big Eats and Little Eats), and Tom's parentage was much discussed in the privacy of the lavatory (Ploppers). Montmorency had been in the building for less than an hour when a keen new member, showing – to Montmorency's experienced eye – all the signs of working in the secret side of government service, sidled up to him with hints of interesting missions that might come his way. Remembering his pledge to Mary, Montmorency pretended not to understand.

The club put Montmorency in his old room on the top floor. On the first morning, he returned from breakfast to find a parcel on the bed, forwarded from the American Embassy. It contained the clothes that had been found in the lodging house where Malpensa had spent his last night on earth. The dark floppy hat was there, and the big cape, still carrying an odour Montmorency recognised from long ago. Montmorency pondered the meaning of this unexpectedly generous gesture from Armitage, who included a note expressing the hope that these objects might serve as tangible reminders that Montmorency's old enemy was gone for good. Was it well meant, or yet another indication to Montmorency that Armitage knew where he was, and might make use of him at any time? Montmorency chided himself for being so suspicious, and took the opportunity to draw a line under their unfortunate relationship. He sent a cable of thanks, adding that there should be no hard feelings now that the affair was over. While he was at the telegraph office, he dispatched another message to Alexander in Washington, to let him know that all was well, and a third to Mary, regretting that no letter had reached London yet, and hoping that she would soon join him for their wedding.

The next day, one of the Sams brought two replies. The first was from Alexander, with the exciting news that Angelina was probably expecting twins, who, if they were boys, would be called George (after the late Lord George Fox-Selwyn) and Xavier, after Montmorency himself. Montmorency flinched at the reminder of his embarrassing first name, coined during a drunken session in Big Drinks long ago.

The other cable was from Mary. It said she would not be coming to London. She was formally releasing Montmorency from any promises he had made. She was sure he would understand that, after the recent cooling of their friendship, she felt Harrison Bayfield would be a better choice of husband. Harrison genuinely needed her, and would appreciate her love and support. They were leaving Paterson immediately, and would be married without delay.

Montmorency's hands shook as he read and re-read the message, hoping he had misunderstood. But the meaning was clear, and the inevitably curt tone of the telegram made it clearer still. By sending the news in such a way, Mary showed she truly believed that Montmorency's love had died. Montmorency knew she would never be so cruel as to reject a true admirer by cable. And she spoke of Bayfield's need for her, without acknowledging Montmorency's own protestations of devotion and dependency in his many letters. He was left in no doubt that Armitage had sabotaged all his attempts to explain his behaviour during those last dangerous days in Paterson. Mary must have been left in the dark about his disappearance after the parade.

Montmorency could see that his own staccato message, more than a fortnight later, breaking the news that he was happily in London, would have told of a cowardly attempt to escape from her. Mary must have seen it as yet another manifestation of the selfishness he had exhibited in recent weeks. Viewed though that prism, the mention of marriage in his telegram must have appeared to be no more than a reluctant acknowledgement of an implied offer, sent from afar in the hope that it would be declined with dignity.

Montmorency read Mary's message again, though he knew it by heart already. She did not say where she and Bayfield were going. There was no way to put things right. By the time Montmorency found her, she would be a married woman. He cursed Jerrold Armitage. Of course, there was no reply from him. How bitterly Montmorency regretted his generous declaration of 'no hard feelings' now.

There was a knock on the door. It was Frank.

"The chef wants to know if we approve of the menu for dinner tonight," he said, handing Montmorency a note. "They're letting us have Little Eats all to ourselves, to mark your return – and so the members aren't outraged by the presence of ladies, of course. We'll have to make sure that Vi keeps her voice down!"

"Looks fine to me," said Montmorency, though in truth he could barely see the words on the menu for the moisture in his eyes.

"I never thought I'd look forward to seeing Dad but, do you know, I can't wait for him to get here!" said Frank, taking the slip of paper back. "Are you sure beef is a good idea? They'll have been eating the very best Aberdeen Angus up in Scotland. I wouldn't want them to be disappointed, tonight of all nights."

"You're right. Pork would be better. What time does their train get in?" said Montmorency mechanically, though he couldn't have been less interested in the answer.

"Four o'clock. I thought I'd go up to meet them with Tom. He'll be glad to see his mother after so long away from her. Thank heavens she never knew he was missing."

"Yes. We'll all be pleased to see Vi. And Gus and Beatrice, too, of course."

"And we can all drink to the death of Malpensa, at last," said Frank. "You must show them the cape and hat. They'll love them. It will be one of the great nights. So I'll tell the kitchen we'd prefer pork?"

"That's right," said Montmorency, who had turned away, pretending to be occupied with the box of Malpensa's clothes.

"Do you want to come to the station too?"

"I don't think so. I wouldn't want to get in Tom's way when he greets his mother. He'll probably want to go with her to her hotel. I'll meet you all in Little Eats – about 7.30?"

"Perfect. I'll tell Robert on my way down to the chef."

Montmorency was pleased to have engineered an afternoon alone. He imagined the reunion of Tom and Vi, and of Gus, Beatrice and Frank. They would be ecstatic about Alexander's expected twins. Happy family life was all around, except for him. Maybe he should just leave them to it tonight, and let them enjoy their time together, bonded by ties of flesh and blood. He could say he was ill, or even tell the truth, and show them Mary's telegram. But he knew they would be desperate to hear the story of how Malpensa had at last been vanquished, and that Beatrice and Vi would be full of ideas for an Italian holiday, so everyone could bask in sunshine and freedom from fear. They would expect him to be part of it all.

Montmorency picked up his old opera hat, opening and closing it as he turned over in his mind every option from suicide to pretending that all was well. He looked out of the window and saw Robert Farcett, walking alone in the park far below. Dear old Robert, who had been through so much grief and pain since he had thrown away his own chance of married bliss. Robert, who had saved Montmorency's life, and who had so nearly lost his own to uncontrolled grief. At last Montmorency fully understood his old friend. Montmorency had felt physical pain and even self-loathing many times, but never this agonising mix of despair, regret, anger, and humiliation. He squashed the crown of the hat down, and let it spring up again.

On the next push, there was a snap, and the folding mechanism flopped out of its frame, leaving him with a handful of useless silk. His favourite hat was no more. It had accompanied him from one life to another, and now he was on his own. At last the dam broke. He threw himself onto the bed and cried until sleep numbed his misery.

When Frank and Tom returned and hammered on Montmorency's door to make sure he was getting ready, he tried saying that he felt unwell. Tom walked straight in to find out what was wrong, and refused to let him cry off dinner.

"You just have to come, Dad. You must. I know Mum's dying to see you. She's in spectacular form. She's got a new hat with feathers and a veil, and she's brought you a present from Scotland. I think it might be a kilt. Come on Dad. We'll have a really happy time. It's important to bring everyone back together again."

Everyone except Mary, thought Montmorency, but he could see that his own son didn't even notice her absence, or think of her as a vital component of his life. Tom's real family was that strange assortment of classes and backgrounds thrown together by Montmorency's own bizarre progress though the world.

As if to echo his thoughts, Tom nagged on, "We need you, Dad. You're the one who knits us all together."

Montmorency was determined not to let Tom down, yet again. Tonight would be a joyous occasion for everyone else, and Montmorency had a responsibility to them. He would hide his true emotions, just as he had disguised so many things about himself for more than twenty years. He had to go on, for Tom's sake, for Frank and Robert, and for everybody whose lives had been shaped, for good or ill, by things he had done, and decisions he had made.

"I'll see you downstairs, then," he said to Tom. "Tell everyone I won't be long."

"You'd better not be. The others will be here soon, and if you keep dinner waiting, Mum will have a bit too much champagne. You know what she can be like!"

Do I? Montmorency thought. In his obsession with Mary he had almost forgotten Vi, whom he had first seen as a grubby teenager sitting outside a sleazy boarding house in Covent Garden. Now she was housekeeper, and friend, to a duke and duchess. And Gus and Beatrice were rebuilding their lives too. Their grief over George's death would soon take second place to grandparental pride. Tom was right. Montmorency owed these old friends their moment of joy.

He opened his wardrobe to choose the clothes he would wear to dinner: the smart tail coat, the French waistcoat, the Italian silk cravat, and the cufflinks and shirt studs that had once belonged to dear George Fox-Selwyn. Tonight he would dress up, and smile. No one would know the truth.

At the bottom of the stairs he paused to prepare for his entrance, swallowing hard to stave off tears. The swing doors to Little Eats had glass panels, etched with swirling floral designs. Looking though a clear patch, Montmorency caught glimpses of the jollity within. His friends were all still standing, waiting for him to arrive. Gus was in one corner with Frank, apparently deep in conversation, but they both suddenly roared at what must have been one of Frank's risqué jokes, and the Duchess flapped her fan in mock outrage. Vi was holding out one arm to get her glass refilled while with the other she hugged her handsome son. Tom broke away from her embrace to tell a story of his own. Montmorency couldn't hear it, but he could tell from the actions that it was a perfect parody of one of Fregoli's turns. Soon everyone was laughing, and Frank, seizing Beatrice's fan, joined in, playing the part of a demure heroine.

Someone slapped Montmorency on the shoulder.

"Coming for a drink?" said the secret service man whose overtures he had turned down the day before.

"Sorry, I'm going in here. Private Party. Family reunion," said Montmorency.

"Don't let me hold you up," said the man, taking a peek through the glass. "It looks like fun. But here's my card, in case you want to get in touch." He smiled. "The name's Fraser, Christopher Fraser."

Montmorency twiddled the card between his fingers without reading the address. He looked around for a waste paper basket, but there was none to be seen.

"Well done in America, by the way," Fraser said, as he made for the bar. "Good work."

Montmorency could have done without the reminder of everything he was trying to forget. He waited for a moment, wondering whether to go back upstairs. There was another peal of laughter from the dining room. Vi was trying to persuade Robert Farcett to dance. Montmorency tucked Fraser's card into his waistcoat pocket, breathed deeply, and pushed on the door.

"Here he is!" shouted Tom, as the others cheered. "Get him a drink".

"What took you so long?" Frank asked, as Montmorency kissed Beatrice on the cheek, and shook hands with Gus.

"Oh, you know me," said Montmorency. "A little last-minute titivating never goes amiss on an occasion like this."

"I think you look a treat," said Vi. "Now, let's all sit down, and you can tell us how you saw off Malpensa!"

"No, I want all your news first," said Montmorency. "I haven't heard your voices for such a long time."

So he sat through the soup and fish listening to his old friends blathering about their lives in Scotland, and their plans for a spring holiday. Eventually, he had to tell his own tale. Frank, Tom and Farcett unknowingly helped him out by interrupting and taking over the story, and Tom leapt at the chance to be the one who showed off Malpensa's clothes. Montmorency had to call on all his powers of deception to seem as happy and relaxed as the rest of them, but no one guessed that his smiles masked the greatest pain he had ever felt. From time to time he checked his waistcoat pocket, to make sure that Fraser's card was still there. Maybe he would meet him – just for a drink. It couldn't do any harm.

At the end of the evening, after he had seen Gus, Beatrice and Vi back to their hotel, Montmorency wandered alone up to Covent Garden. The opera fans had left for the night, and the market traders had not yet arrived. Vi's old boarding house was still standing, even more run down than when he had lived there as Scarper, storing stolen jewels under the floorboards. He walked to the Strand, found a cab, and asked to be taken to the Marimion Hotel, where he had transformed himself into the man his friends recognised today. The driver told him it was closed for renovation. Montmorency rather liked the phrase. *Maybe I should close for renovation, too,* he thought. *Or demolition, perhaps.*

"Just drive me around," he said. "I've been away for a while. I want to see how the city has changed."

While the cab wove its way through the dark streets, Montmorency contemplated his future. Should he return to

America and search for Mary? He pictured Tom's face if he said he was leaving, Mary's anguish if he tried to tear her away from her new husband, and his own response should he run in to Armitage. He knew he wouldn't go. He wondered how to tell his friends that he wasn't getting married after all. He knew Farcett would be disappointed – he had viewed the prospect of Montmorency's happiness as a recompense for his own failure. But would the others really care that much? Had anyone even asked about Mary over dinner? He was rather offended that they hadn't, although relieved to be spared a direct challenge to his confected bonhomie. Maybe he should just continue to pretend. After all, as Frank had once shouted in a rage, deception was what Montmorency did best. But what if he just told his friends the truth, and asked them to help him find a way to continue without the woman he loved? After living with so many lies in Paterson, it would be a relief to be himself again – whoever that was.

The cab turned onto Piccadilly. He wasn't far from Bargles now.

"I can get out and walk from here," said Montmorency, reaching for his wallet. "I'm almost home."

He stepped from the cab and strode off for the club. Big Ben struck the quarter hour, and a passing car splashed his trousers with mud as it sped through a puddle.

Montmorency was back in London. He was broken-hearted, but at least he was still alive.

ABOUT THE AUTHOR

Eleanor Updale's books are enjoyed by children and adults alike. They have won prizes on both sides of the Atlantic, including the *Blue Peter Award for The Book I Couldn't Put Down*, the *Silver Smarties Prize*, and *The Fantastic Book Award*. Eleanor has been longlisted and shortlisted for many major book awards, including the *Carnegie Medal* and the *Guardian Prize*.

Born in London, she now spends most of her time in Edinburgh.

BOOKS BY ELEANOR UPDALE

Montmorency
Montmorency on the Rocks
Montmorency and the Assassins
Montmorency's Revenge
Montmorency Returns

Johnny Swanson

The Last Minute

Saved

And numerous contributions to compilations of short stories: see www.eleanorupdale.com

.

Made in the USA
Las Vegas, NV
04 January 2023

64384445R00118